THE LIBERATION OF
MARGARET McCABE

CATHERINE BROPHY was born in Dublin. As a student in UCD, she discovered hitch-hiking in Europe and beyond. Since then she's taught in Mexico, sewn curtains in Vienna, dug trenches in Turkey, lectured in Los Angeles, got lost with a circus troupe in Yugoslavia and been kitchen-maid in a works canteen in Mill Hill. Back in Ireland she's worked with children who have hearing losses. At last it dawned on her that she wasn't going to win the Sweep or marry a millionaire, so she chained herself to the typewriter instead. The result is *The Liberation of Margaret McCabe*.

I'd like to thank all my friends who encouraged me to go on writing. A very special thanks to Nuala Rothery, who not only encouraged me but typed the manuscript as well. Thanks also to my editor Jeanne Marie Finlay for her invaluable advice.

The
LIBERATION
of
MARGARET McCABE

Catherine Brophy

Wolfhound Press

First published 1985 by
WOLFHOUND PRESS
68 Mountjoy Square, Dublin 1.

All characters in this novel are fictitious and any apparent similarities to any persons living or dead are coincidental.

This book is published with the assistance of
The Arts Council (An Comhairle Ealaíon),
Dublin, Ireland.

British Library Cataloguing in Publication Data

Brophy, Catherine
  The liberation of Margaret McCabe.
  I. Title
823'.914[F]   PR6052.R58/

ISBN 0-86327-068-9
ISBN 0-86327-067-0 Pbk

Cover illustration: *Woman at her Window* by Pauline Bewick. By kind permission of the artist and with acknowledgement to Arbutus Lodge Hotel, Montenotte, Cork.
Typesetting: Redsetter Ltd., Dublin.

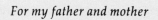

For my father and mother

1

HE'D SAID IT AGAIN!

What the hell does he think I'm made of? Granite? I'll kill him! I ground my teeth in the effort to keep quiet.

What he had said was: 'I used to have this Japanese girlfriend. Christ! She was amazing . . . fantastic. . . .' He'd smiled reminiscently, raising his head slowly from *The Financial Times.* 'And she looked so demure too, a bit like you, only in bed she was something else. . . .' He'd chuckled and rattled the paper.

It must have been at least the millionth time he'd told me about her since I'd come to live with him eight months ago. But he never said what it was she did that was so amazing and fantastic.

I sighed and felt inadequate. It's true, I thought, I don't have all that much experience in bed; Oliver is the first man I've ever slept with, but I'm extremely well read, and nobody could fault my enthusiasm.

'Ten out of ten for enthusiasm,' Oliver had said another night, 'and seven-point-five for performance.' It was the seven-point-five that rankled. I bought a copy of *The Joy of Sex* and read it very carefully. It didn't work. Every time I tried seduction on the sofa it was sabotaged by the television. Oliver would get a hint of a news programme, a discussion on the arms race, a football match, and he'd go rigid, tell me to hush, and stare fixedly over my shoulder at the screen. When I made my moves in bed I had to wade through *Newsweek, Time* and the daily newspapers to get at his body. Usually Oliver grabbed my hand, imprisoned it on his chest, and muttered: 'Just a minute, just a minute.' Ages later, when I'd hear the magazine fall plop on the floor, I'd have to take off his glasses, cover his shoulders and turn off the light.

What the hell did that Japanese girlfriend do anyway? 'Oliver,

I wish you'd tell me some of those Japanese techniques,' I said quietly.

He rattled the pink pages and continued as though he hadn't heard my question. 'You see, Margaret, Japanese men have such little sex drive that the women have to get up to some pretty amazing tricks to get them started.' He turned to the next page.

I bet they don't have to compete with fifteen tons of newsprint, I thought nastily, but I didn't want to divert him from the main point. 'Oliver,' I persisted, 'did you hear what I said?'

He sighed, took off his glasses, laid down his paper, and looked martyred. 'Well?'

'Well, it's just that you keep talking about her, the Japanese one, and, well . . . well, I know I don't have much experience, but why don't you show me what to do? I . . . I . . .', I petered out.

'Oh, don't be ridiculous Mag. You're just being hypersensitive.' He put on his glasses and took up the paper again.

I drew a long, slow breath and fiddled with the edge of the duvet.

'And besides,' he continued, 'of all the women I've known, I'd certainly put you in the top ten. Say about sixth or seventh.' He gave his complete attention to debentures and consols now that my objections had been dealt with.

Top ten indeed! If they're all so great where are they now? And I don't want to be sixth or seventh.

But I didn't say any of this out loud. He didn't like women who made a fuss. He'd often told me that was one of the things he liked most about me: that I was calm and didn't make a fuss and a row like some women he'd known. So instead of saying anything to him, I concentrated on piercing him with imaginary poison darts. After a while I got tired of that and turned over, pulling as much of the duvet as possible around me in the hope that I'd disturb his papers. I moved as close to my side of the bed as possible without actually putting my head on the bedside table. I didn't want any part of me to touch him.

I mean, seven-point-five and sixth or seventh place. It's not fair. I just amn't going to touch him. He is going to have to make the first move. He must know how I feel now. He absolutely must. I'd made it plain as plain.

But if he did, he wasn't letting on. Eventually, I heard the thud of his papers falling on the floor. I turned out the light, but I didn't take off his glasses, nor did I cover his shoulders. I wished him a severe crick in his neck and turned over to try and sleep. Then he started to snore.

Next morning, Oliver was disappointingly supple, with no crick in his neck. I was still feeling prickly. I said nothing and only answered the barest minimum when he spoke first. He didn't seem to notice, or maybe he was waiting for it all to blow over.

In any event I was not at my sunniest when I got in to the school where I teach and was greeted by Sister Magdalen, the Principal. She gave me one of her saintly smiles accompanied by the barest hint of a glance at her pocket watch. It let me know that even if I wasn't late, I was only barely on time. She had a whole range of little tricks like that to make you feel permanently at a disadvantage.

That woman drives me mad. She's a hatchet. A lethal, double-edged, all steel hatchet. Not that you'd know that by just looking at her. She is tall and elegant, with kindly, twinkling blue eyes and a madonna-shaped face. She looks remarkably like the statue of Our Lady in the school chapel, and knows it. When the order changed their floor-length skirts for shorter, more practical clothes, she refused to change. Only Sister Magdalen and few of the really ancient nuns persist in wearing the long white habit with the blue veil and the soft, white shoes we call convent creepers. 'It's the habit which Our Lady gave to our foundress in a miraculous vision,' she would say demurely, 'and I hope to continue wearing it for my lifetime.' To which Nora Harvey would mutter under her breath: 'And maybe you'd like to climb on a bush and be a miraculous vision yourself!' But then, Nora has been on the staff longer than anybody else, and she is very cynical, very bitter. I'm not nearly as bad.

Sister Magdalen is the darling of the media. Without her, no serious discussion about the future of education could take place on radio or television. She is a fabulous speaker and a natural for television. When she speaks at a conference she provokes both public and private panegyrics about the wonderful work which the nuns do in education, especially in the education of the deprived, the poor and the handicapped. It drives some of us lay teachers mad, because we're the ones who are actually doing the wonderful work, Sister Magdalen is just talking about it.

The parents of the children think she's wonderful too. The children don't though, but maybe that's because of the kind of school it is. St Brigid's Special School for Emotionally Disturbed Girls – which is a nice way of putting it – is a reformatory for girls who have been in trouble with the law. It used to be a large gloomy building surrounded by high walls. The children were fed on brown windsor soup and elderly cabbage, and kept in line by rules and punishments. Then Sister Magdalen came along. She decided that the girls were not criminals, but special children, needing special treatment and special care. The walls came down. The big, gloomy dormitories were divided up with brightly painted cubicles, the refectory was broken up into dining areas with formica-topped tables, and plants were placed on every windowsill. Sister Magdalen started recruiting young lay teachers for the school who would give the girls the loving teaching which they needed. In spite of all this, however, the girls are still kept in line by rules and punishments and the food has stayed the same.

The teachers are divided in their opinions of Sister Magdalen. Those who never have a row with her think she is wonderful; those who have know better. But if you've experience only of her charm it is impossible to believe how nasty she can be. She can certainly be very, very charming.

The moment I stepped into my classroom that morning I knew there was something wrong. It was probably Patricia Walsh. Feared and respected by the other girls even though only twelve and a bit, Patricia comes from a long line of criminals and her own speciality is car thefts and terrorising old women into giving up their handbags and, though very sweet and lovable, she needs the constant excitement of trouble. But I looked over at Mary Haverty instead because she was rocking frantically backwards and forwards. She is my barometer: the harder she rocks the more trouble there is likely to be. She can hear and understand normally, but has chosen not to speak for the last five years.

The morning passed, however, and nothing unusual

happened. There were one or two outbursts of screaming tempers, but that's something you get used to in this school, so I let them go and vent their anger on the huge fat cushion I keep in the classroom for that purpose.

Sister Magdalen passed while Patricia was doing some noisy cushion bashing; as she glanced through the glass in the door I saw the look of disapproval, but she went on without comment. She doesn't really approve of that cushion: she thinks the girls should learn to control their tempers. 'What would visitors think if they heard the noise?' Fortunately, one day an eminent visitor told her it was a good idea, so she now accepts the theory, but I don't think she will ever accept the practice.

After lunch the tension was still there and Mary was still rocking like crazy. There were expectant looks on their faces.

Pat Walsh put up her hand and looked innocent. 'Please, miss,' she said, her eyes wide and blue, 'will you tell us where babies come from?'

'Certainly, Pat. What would you like to know?'

'Well, miss, we all know that babies come from inside their mammies, but how do they get there?' She sat down, smiling sweetly and batting her eyes.

Round the class there were uncontrollable bursts of sniggles. Angela Flynn dropped a biro and chortled to the floorboards. Andrea Matthews and Pearl King snatched up their desk lids and tee-heed. Everyone except Pat was avoiding my eye.

I drew some diagrams on the board, explained male and female genital anatomy and showed them exactly how the sperm fertilised the ovum. I had instant attention. They were fascinated and had hundreds of questions. Even Pat took the bland look off her face and joined in. For kids who were so street-wise and hard-boiled, they seemed just as ignorant of the facts of reproduction as I had been at their age. When half past three came they were still quizzing me. I left the classroom feeling that I had done a good day's work.

I was always home well before Oliver, so that evening I had plenty of time to decide what my strategy should be. I thought of continuing the speak-only-when-spoken-to routine, but that seemed somehow childish. What if he never noticed what I was doing and we continued like that for the rest of our lives? No, no, that was too like some of the depressing mid-week plays they have on the BBC. Eventually, I decided that I would just stick to my side of the bed. No matter what happened I would not touch him. I wouldn't kiss him or touch him at all. Not unless he did it first. I always had to start things, but this time he'd have to make the first move. Surely he'd notice that, I mean he couldn't be that insensitive.

Oliver came home needing lots of care and attention. Nothing all that ghastly had happened to him, but he did make the car stalling twice at a traffic light seem like a major catastrophe. We ate, watched television and went to bed. He read *Business and Finance* until he fell asleep. I said nothing, kept to my own side of the bed and turned off the light as he began to snore. I took some pleasure in tweaking his nose to stop the snores. It only worked for about three minutes. I lay there thinking.

*   *   *

Mrs McIlroy was my very first teacher. Because I was the youngest, my mother kept me home till I was six, so I started school in High Infants. The classroom door opened to my mother's knock, and I got my first view of a teacher. Well not exactly my first view, because my friend Mairín's mammy was a teacher; but that was different, as any time I saw her she was just being a mammy.

Mrs McIlroy was large and had that smooth upholstered look that comes from quality corseting; her huge, sloping, cherry-red bosom reminded me of Mother Hen; her peach-coloured face-powder made a floury line round her jaw; the slash of red lipstick – my mother had told me that bright lipstick and red clothes were vulgar, and no vulgarity was allowed in our house – was leaking into little lines round her mouth; there was a yellow streak in her hair and a smell of cigarettes off her. She was not my idea of a teacher at all. From everything I'd heard at home I knew that teachers were very important people who knew an awful lot. I had expected my teacher to be elegant and serious; I thought she would wear a dimanté brooch and a good dress like my mother did for special occasions. But Mrs McIlroy wasn't like that at all.

'So this is your youngest, Mrs McCabe,' said my new teacher and held out her hand to me.

'Yes, this is Margaret.' Mammy smiled and nudged me forward. 'Shake hands with Mrs McIlroy, Margaret.'

Mrs McIlroy took my hand, made me say goodbye to my mother and led me into her classroom. I saw rows and rows of little girls, heads bobbing, curls and plaits swirling as they laughed and talked together.

'Ciuineas, a chailíní,' she clapped her hands for silence, 'quiet now girls.' During the scuffling which followed, she brought me over to one of the desks in the front row and introduced me to Nora Paxton. 'You can be Margaret's guardian angel, Nora,' she said.

My guardian angel squinted at me. She was a thin, pale-faced girl with dry skin. Her wispy, straight, mousey hair hung into her gooseberry coloured eyes. Her thin blue cardigan was stained and a safety pin replaced one of the buttons.

Then Mrs McIlroy went to hang a long string of painted wooden spools across the room. She talked to the class and moved the spools up and down the string. I really couldn't follow what she was saying, I was too busy taking in the strangeness of it all. Then she told us to do it in our jotters. I didn't know what 'it' was.

'How do you do it?' I asked Nora.

'You do it with liaroidí, balls, in your jotter, but you can do it with your fingers under the desk, only you're not supposed to,' she whispered back.

She bent her head close to her book and began muttering and frowning to herself. Now and again she'd take a surreptitious look at her fingers under the desk. I was intrigued and impressed when Nora made little dots on her page and then wrote down numbers. I wondered if I'd ever be able to master this mystery. But when Mrs McIlroy came round to look, she told Nora that her sums were all wrong and that she'd have to do them again.

Nora and her friends Barbara and Norma became my friends too, all the way through High Infants, First Class and into Seniors. It was from them that I learned to tie a thread to a door knocker and bang on it from a distance. I always held my breath when the woman of the house stuck out her hair-netted head, looked up and down the street and, muttering, withdrew again. I was sure that sometime we'd be caught and I couldn't imagine what punishment my parents would give me if they were told what I'd done. The others thought it was all great fun and couldn't care less if they were caught. Their parents would only mind if it was a policeman or a schools' attendance officer who came complaining to the house, because they could send them to jail, but their parents never listened to an 'aul' wan' like that. The girls brought me scutting on lorries and taught me how to distract the assistant's attention at the sweet counter in Woolworth's while they stole toffees. They knew the best places to go if you wanted to mitch from school. Once they even pulled a hair from the tail of the slopman's horse while it stood between the shafts of the cart. They assured me that a horse's hair across the palm would stop the pain if the teacher caned me. I thought they led very exotic lives and were let do all kinds of things which were forbidden to me. I wished and wished and wished that I lived in a home where I could read comics and where uncles would give me money every Saturday.

I often begged my mother to let me wear summer dresses and short socks to school in winter; everyone else in my class did. But she said it was only because they were poor and couldn't afford better and that I should thank my lucky stars I had parents who didn't spend money on drink and cigarettes and could look after me properly.

She was always at pains to remind us of our heritage which, according to her, was a cut above buttermilk – her family were the Hanrattys of Carraig-on-Shannon who owned shops all over Leitrim, and my father had a brilliant mind and a good job in the Civil Service, though his people were only small farmers – 'Always remember who you are and behave yourselves,' she used to say to Lucy, Patrick and me whenever we were going out visiting.

On one occasion I tried asking for hornpipe shoes but my mother reminded me that they were vulgar, and in any event were only made of cardboard and wouldn't last a wet week. I wasn't allowed have money for sweets because they were bad for my teeth and would spoil my appetite. And when I complained I was told that there was many a poor starving child in China who would be only too grateful for the nutritious cabbage, brown windsor soup and tapioca pudding which I didn't want to eat. And as for reading comics!

'Comics is it? Reading comics!' exploded my father when Patrick brought some home from school. Daddy took them from him and leafed through them, shaking his dark, greying head in disapproval. 'English and American trash, that's all this is. Written for illiterates by illiterates. No decent Irish person would be bothered reading the likes of that. If it's reading you want there's plenty of good reading in the classics.' Then he began to quote a long bit of *Paradise Lost*.

Reluctantly I wore to school my sensible dresses with plenty of letting down in them and my sensible brown, laced shoes. In winter I put on brown, ribbed stockings with the horrible elastic garters that were always breaking and having to be tied again in painful knots. My only disobedience was to borrow comics and smuggle them home stuck up the leg of my knickers, hoping that the leg-elastic wouldn't give as I slipped through the kitchen past my mother. Under the blankets at night, by the ochre light of a torch, I read all the adventures of Desperate Dan and Beryl the Peril. The only way I could get pocket money was to pretend on the bus home from school that I'd lost my fare and throw myself on the conductor's mercy. Sometimes a kindly neighbour, returning from town, would take pity on me and pay, sometimes the conductor would make me get off the bus and tell me to walk. It was worth it though, to have pennies to saunter down to Lyon's corner shop and lean on the shiny brown counter, trying to decide between gobstoppers and lucky lumps or sticky candy.

In the school playground Barbara showed me how to play 'One, two, three O'Leary' against the end wall of the bicycle shed. Barbara was tall for her age and had silvery blonde sausage curls. Her bright blue eyes were like a doll's in her pink and white, strong-jawed face. She frowned a lot, which made her look serious, and she had epileptic fits. Any time the teacher made her stand at the side of the classroom for not knowing her lessons, Barbara's eyes would roll up in her head and she'd fall on the floor in a dead faint. Then the teacher would have to let her sit down. One time she even pee'd on the floor at the same time so the teacher had to send her home and wipe up the floor after her.

Everyone in the class thought she was dead lucky to be able to do that. At home I tried practising falling like that but at the last second I'd always have to take a step to break my fall.

'My daddy is bringing me a big sleeping doll for Christmas,' Barbara said as she handed Norma the rubber balls for her to take her turn. 'He works in England and comes home on a huge big boat.' She flicked back her fat curls with pride.

'My da works in Jacob's and can get loads and loads of free biscuits,' said Norma.

'That's nothing,' interrupted Nora, 'my daddy is a soldier in the army and he has a gun. We live in the married quarters so if robbers come my daddy can shoot them!'

I thought of my father, tall and thin in his grey suit and beige mackintosh, waving goodbye to us as he cycled off to his office and I knew I just couldn't compete. Then I remembered Joe the Coalman. He came down our road every Thursday selling coal from a horse-drawn cart. He rang a handbell and called out, 'Coal. Coaaaal, get your Cooaaal!' As he called, front doors opened and women came out waving their purses to attract his attention and we children gathered round to admire the horse. The last time Joe had come round my brother Patrick and my best friend Mairín Weldon sat on the kerb to watch the horse. Lucy, my snooty elder sister, and her precious friend Maeve wouldn't join us. 'You'll get your clothes all dirty and Mammy'll kill you,' Lucy had warned. Mammy always said that Lucy was a rock of sense but I just thought she was a spoilsport; her and her silly friend, all they ever did was read books and be sensible. Joe's horse was old and slow and bony but ever so often it would snort and shake its head and bare its dirty yellow teeth at us. Mairín and I screamed and clutched one another and Patrick, older, male, laughed at our fears. As we sat there anticipating the next scare, the horse did a long, fascinating, glittering yellow piss, right there in front of us. The steaming liquid foamed and flowed and pushed the dust around in the gutter. Then came the plop, plop of brown, straw-flecked droppings, strong smelling and spicy. To top it all, the horse flung back its head, shook its mane and whinnied. Joe sat on top of a pile of black sacks. His clothes and his cap were black. His face was dirty grey and the lines on it looked as though they had been drawn with a black crayon. His hands were filthy and his nails were black. I thought it must be wonderful to be allowed to be that dirty and sit on a pile of sacks driving a horse and cart. When Joe and his horse moved on my mother mortified me by coming out with a brush and shovel and the horse droppings became respectable manure for her roses.

'Well, my daddy is a coalman,' I boasted, 'and he has a horse and cart and he keeps them in a shed at the bottom of the garden.'

'I don't believe you,' challenged Nora.

'Yes he is, he is,' I protested, 'and anyway I don't believe that your daddy has a gun.'

'Well why don't you come with me after school and you can see for yourself.'

After school I went with Nora to the barracks where she lived. As we came closer I saw the soldiers outside the huge green gate. She was right about the guns, I could see them.

'Why are they standing like that at the gate?' I asked her.

'To keep out enemies,' she replied seriously.

I hoped that they wouldn't think I was an enemy.

Once past the gate, we had to cross a huge square with flower-beds in the middle. There was a small group of soldiers marching past with rifles on their shoulders and an officer in front shouting things I couldn't make out.

'There's my daddy, there.' Nora pointed excitedly at the group. 'Where? Where?'

'Right there, in the middle.'

But I couldn't make out which one he was.

When I got home that evening I told my mother where I'd been. 'You know you're to come straight home from school,' she scolded. 'I don't want you to go there again.'

'But soldiers fight enemies and robbers,' I reminded her. 'And anyway wasn't daddy a soldier one time?'

'Yes well, but that was different. He was an officer and it was during the Emergency.'

That sounded a lot better than just working in an office. It sounded like it might be something to do with Pádraigh Pearse and 1916 and Ireland fighting for freedom against England. Later I told a teacher during a history class that my daddy had fought for Irish freedom during the Emergency. She smiled and told me that she thought he'd have been far too young, that the Emergency was about England and France fighting against Hitler's Germany and anyway Ireland wasn't fighting at the time.

I never went back to see the soldiers in the barracks but when Norma suggested that I go to her house, to see her banister, I forgot all about delaying on the way home. Although Norma was one of my group of pals I felt a bit shy of her, she seemed so confident with her dark bunches of ringlets done up in shiny satin bows and her olive skin and brown eyes. She gave cheek to the teachers and often she didn't have her homework done. Her behaviour both scandalised and thrilled me. But, best of all, she had steel tips on the soles and heels of her patent leather shoes and had won prizes for tap-dancing.

'We have a huge long banister in our house and you can slide all the way down from the very top of the house to the very bottom without getting off.'

It sounded wonderful.

'Do you want to see it?'

'Wouldn't your mammy mind?' I asked.

'No she wouldn't. Anyway she's out at work.'

Norma lived in the top flat in a tall narrow house. There were three storeys over the basement and steps leading up to the front door. The hall was dark and bare and smelled stale, but there was the banister, just as she had promised. It was the longest banister I'd ever seen, gleaming a dull golden brown in the dim hall.

'Come on, I'll race you to the top,' said Norma, and she started up the stairs three at a time.

She beat me easily and was sitting on the top step looking smug when I dragged myself up the last steps panting. To my astonishment she jumped side-saddle onto the banister and slid all the way to the bottom, not even slowing down for the turns. I leaned over the rail to watch her and her daring left me with my mouth open.

'Come on, what's keeping you?' she called up from the hall below.

I tried to hitch myself up on one haunch but when I looked over at the huge drop to the basement I got frightened. I was too used to being careful like my mother always told me. So I slid down the ordinary way and even then had to get off at the turns. Norma tried to show me how she did it but nothing she could tell me would give me her cool, confident nerve.

After a while we just sat on the top step and talked. There seemed to be nobody at all in the big, dim house. She told me that her mammy and her sister worked in the Twilfit corset factory, so when they got paid on Friday they brought home fish and chips from the chipper, and gave her money to buy sweets and go to the pictures on Saturday. She showed me the cups she had won for tap-dancing and did three of the dances, singing the tunes as she bobbed up and down. I was entranced. I loved the way her curls bounced as she danced, but most of all I loved the way her toes and heels went ticky-tack-tick-tack-tack-tick on the hard floor. She taught me some of the steps but it wasn't the same without the tips on my shoes.

It was nearly dark when I got home and mammy was both furious and relieved. 'How many times have I to tell you, Margaret, that you're to come straight home from school? I don't want you hanging round tenements and barracks, anything could happen. What's wrong with the friends you have at home? Why can't you come home and play with Mairín?'

Later, after our meal, we were all sitting round the table, the dishes still unwashed, with a feeling of family comfort.

'Mam, can I learn tap-dancing?' I inquired.

There was no answer.

'Please, Mam, can I?'

'No indeed you cannot.'

'Aw Mam!' I whined.

'Tap-dancing is it?' asked my father, lowering his *Evening Mail* to look me straight in the eye over the top of his reading glasses. 'Tap-dancing is all very well and fine for the ones who act in the pictures but they only do it because they haven't got the brains for anything better. I expect a lot more of my family. I hope you children realise the sacrifices your mother and I are making to make sure you get a good education. Just you remember that, Miss Margaret. Tap-dancing indeed!'

He rattled his paper back up in front of him. Lucy looked superior and began virtuously collecting cups and saucers together. Patrick caught my eye and gave me a big wink. I felt like crying. Daddy lowered his paper again.

'I'd much prefer to see you do a decent Irish reel or a hornpipe than that rubbish they put in the pictures. Sure you couldn't call that culture at all.'

So they decided to send me to Irish dancing classes with my friend Mairín. Well it was better than nothing and I knew a girl who lived over in Kilronan Park who got steel tips on her shoes for doing the hornpipe. Maybe after all I could make my feet go ticky-tack-tick, just like Norma.

Though we had not gone to primary school together, Mairín had been my best friend since ever I could remember. We had scraped our knees climbing the same walls and torn our dresses crossing the same forbidden barbed-wire fence. I envied her scooter and she was jealous of my big American doll. We ate in one another's houses, slept in one another's beds and joined one another's families for outings. Because I was so much younger than Patrick and Lucy, my mother encouraged our friendship. She thought Mairín was a very nice polite child, and the fact that both her parents were teachers was an added bonus. She had jet black curly hair pulled back in two fat plaits and tiny curls escaped all round the edge of her forehead. Her eyes were big and grey and I used to jeer her about her freckles. At the time I didn't realise that she was very pretty; she was my best friend and that's all that mattered.

I loved everything about my secondary school: the girls in uniform wearing white veils to sing in the chapel; the ordered way we filed from the study hall to our classrooms; the prints along the corridors, Nativities, Madonnas and saints by Raphael and Murillo in heavy gold frames; the way the nuns had their books neatly covered in brown paper with 'Ad Usum Sr Whoever' written in the right hand corner; the way they swished by in long grey habits, round their faces starched linen like corrugated wrapping paper; writing A.M.D.G., the initials of our school motto, 'For the Greater Glory of God', at the head of every page in my exercise book; the small class and the fact that I was allowed to sit beside Mairín. I thought it was all lovely until Sister Dominic decided that I needed moulding. It was all Mairín's fault really.

We had always shared secrets that adults shouldn't know or else shouldn't know we knew. Like the time we hid in the hedge around the widow's cottage and watched the old lady bend arthritically to take in her milk bottles. We were sure that she must be a witch so we hooted through the privet at her, giving her a fright. Nobody knew either that we practised flying from the lower branches of the huge chestnut in the far corner of the back fields. And no adult could possibly know that we had found out about babies. 'It grows inside the mammy's tummy,' Mairín had told me one afternoon as we sat swinging our legs from a branch of the chestnut after a bout of flight practice. 'But how does it get there?' I asked, not at all sure that she could be right. 'The daddy puts it there of course,' she replied. I had always taken it for granted that babies came out of a large machine on trays, like batch bread from an oven. There'd be doctors there of course to look after the machine and hand out the babies to the waiting parents. 'I don't believe you,' I challenged. 'Cross my heart and hope to die, I swear! Look.' Mairín wet her forefinger and crossed her heart and her throat. Then she continued: 'My mammy told me, but she said not to tell anyone, not even you, because it's a sin to talk about it.' Of course if her mammy told her it was different, she was a teacher and knew nearly every-thing. 'But how does the daddy give it to her?' I persisted. 'I dunno, she didn't tell me that, but I think it must be in a cup of tea,' she hesitated. 'You mean like taking tablets?' I asked. 'Yes, just like that.' I never told anybody about the babies, not even Patrick, although Mairín and I often speculated about it after-wards. And I never, never told about the time the big boys caught us in the back fields and put their hands up our dresses. Mairín said that she told her mammy, but I knew that my mammy would be furious if she knew what had happened.

With secrets like that the joke that Mairín told me didn't seem all that bad. 'Why did Goldilocks run out of the forest?' she asked me on the bus to school one morning. 'I dunno, why?' I replied. 'Because she had a bear behind. Get it? A bare behind!' I got it all right and I laughed because it was rude and rude things were always funny, especially on the bus where strange adults might hear it and be shocked. Adults never thought rude things were funny. At the next bus stop a group of St Saviour's girls joined us. I was dying to tell them the joke but I couldn't because it was Mairín's and she told everybody who would listen. I had to wait till I got home that evening and told it to Patrick.

Next day we had 'Formation' with Sister Dominic. This was the weekly talk to remind us that as pupils of St Saviour's we should never be seen in public without our school berets and gloves, that Our Lady was saddened by slovenly dress, stains on our uniforms, ladders in our stockings and hanging hems. It was always an anxious half-hour: If you didn't sit absolutely erect and pay complete attention, Sister Dominic was likely to come down and poke you in the small of the back with her fountain pen, pull your ears, or, worst of all, bring you to her study for a talking-to. This time she did not watch us file into the study hall, she had her eyes closed. Her fingers delicately held her beads and her lips moved as though in silent prayer. There had to be something wrong. We got to our desks and sat more silently and more erect than usual. She stood motionless, impossibly straight as though she were wearing a steel corset and a canvas webbing posture-improver at the same time. At last she sighed and spoke.

'I have been praying for guidance,' she said, and fell silent again. 'I am ashamed,' she continued at last with her eyes still closed, 'thoroughly ashamed to have to say this to St Saviour's girls.' She lapsed into silence. Then she opened her eyes and looked slowly round the room. 'I understand that some girls were overheard telling . . . unseemly . . . dirty jokes.'

I instantly remembered Mairín's joke, but that wasn't really dirty.

'I want the culprits to own up immediately. In that way they can partially redeem themselves.'

Nobody moved.

'Very well then, if nobody is going to tell the truth I will just have to resort to other methods. Will all those girls who travel on the eighty-eight bus please stay back, the rest of you can go home now.'

I felt a sudden dart of fear in my chest when I realised that I was one of the ones who had to stay back.

When the others had all left, Sister looked silently at each of us in turn. 'Before I go any further, I will give the culprits one last chance to redeem their honour.'

Nobody redeemed honour.

'Very well. Mary Cunningham, come here.'

Mary stumbled out of her desk looking pale and frightened.

'Kneel in front of Our Lady and say this prayer after me.'

Mary knelt in front of the big statue ready to burst into tears.

'Mary Immaculate, conceived without sin, help me to tell the truth,' the nun intoned.

Mary murmured the words after her.

'Stand up.'

Mary stood.

'Did you, Mary Cunningham, tell a dirty joke yesterday?'

'No Sister.'

'Did you then listen to a dirty joke?'

'Yes Sister,' Mary whispered, and she burst into tears.

'Did you protest or object in any way when you heard this joke?' Sister Dominic persisted.

'No Sister.'

'Well, would you like to tell us all who it was who told you this *joke*?' She made the word 'joke' sound like an obscenity.

Mary broke down completely and sobbed. She was in an awful position, she either had to tell on Mairín, and that was unforgivable, or else she had to suffer the nun's wrath if she remained silent. Then Mairín stepped from her desk.

'I told the joke, Sister.'

'Ah Mairín, . . . and why haven't you owned up till now?'

'Because I didn't think it was a dirty joke, Sister.'

'And how exactly would you describe it, Mairín?'

'It might be a bit vulgar, Sister,' she answered, blushing furiously.

Sister Dominic closed her eyes as though bravely bearing excruciating pain. 'Oh child, child! Would you tell such a joke to your parents?'

'Yes Sister.'

The nun's eyes flew open in rage. 'How dare you! You are an evil girl, Mairín Weldon, and a bad bad influence on everybody. I must pray about you before I can decide what punishment is most suitable. Go, go on now out of my sight you abominable child.'

The rest of us were told to go to the chapel and say the rosary
for our sin of having listened to a dirty joke without objecting to
it. On the way out, Sister Dominic beckoned me.

'My office,' she whispered, and signalled for me to follow her.

Dear God, I thought, what have I done? I could think no
farther.

The office was a windowless, odd-shaped little room, the
roofed-over space between higgledy-piggledy additions to the
original buildings. Flat light from a tiny skylight made the
whitewashed walls look cold and dead. There was a pale wooden
crucifix on the wall, a small plain wooden table and two chairs.
She stood directly under the crucifix, placed her missal in the
exact centre of the table, adjusted her habit so that she wouldn't
crush her scapular, and sat down.

'I wish to talk to you about your friendship with Mairín
Weldon,' she said.

'Yes Sister.' I stared fixedly at the splash of liturgical colour
made by the missal's silk markers trailing on to the table.

'I do not think that she is a suitable companion. She
knows . . .', she paused delicately, 'too much for her age. Let us
say that some of her ideas are too mature for her years.'

I said nothing. She said nothing. It was very cold.

'You, Margaret,' she at last continued, 'are an innocent child
and I believe that you should preserve that innocence as long as
possible. Do you understand?'

'Yes Sister,' I said, too paralysed with fright to understand
anything.

'I do not think that you should remain friends. Is that clear?'

Not be friends with Mairín, I couldn't believe it. It was impossible. She couldn't do that!

'I will make arrangements to see that you no longer sit together
in class. Is that clear, Margaret?'

She could do it.

'Yes Sister.'

'I think you have potential, Margaret, but you need to be
moulded.' I didn't think I liked the sound of that either.

Mairín was waiting for me outside the school gates. 'What kept
you?' she asked. 'I've been waiting for ages and ages.'

I told her about Sister Dominic's office and what she had said.

She was angry and tearful. 'I'm going to tell my daddy on her, that's not fair, she shouldn't say those things about me, she's a mean old cow, it's not a bit fair.'

'But what'll Sister say? There's nothing you can do about it.'

'I don't care what she says, I'm going to tell my daddy.'

The next morning on the bus to school she told me that her daddy said he would threaten the law on Sister Dominic for the things she had said about Mairín in front of the school. I couldn't believe that would do any good but he must have done something because Mairín never got any punishment and Sister Dominic made no move to have us separated. Nevertheless, to be on the safe side, I tried my best not to be caught breaking any of her rules.

It was almost a week later before it dawned on me that Sister Dominic must have meant that Mairín knew about babies when she said about knowing too much for her age. I laughed to myself, she didn't realise I knew about them too. It gave me a feeling of evening up the score a bit.

From then on I never seemed to be able to escape Sister Dominic's attention. She noticed every ladder in my stockings, poked my back and lectured me about slouching, quizzed me about attendance at mass during Lent and made my life as miserable as she could. She refused to allow me join the Sodality of the Holy Angels and on Parents' Day she told my mother that she should not give me any information which would spoil my innocence. As a result the Catholic Truth Society pamphlets, *What a Girl Should Know* and *The Devil at Dances*, disappeared from my chest of drawers as mysteriously as they had appeared there. Finally, just as I finished my last year as a junior girl, she confided in me that she believed I might have a vocation to be a nun.

When we returned the following September as seniors, Sister Dominic had gone. She had been given some important-sounding job in the convent and Sister Rose, a neat, no-nonsense little nun with glasses who commanded immediate respect but had no interest at all in catching us out in minor transgressions of perfection, was in charge of the day-pupils; she was much more likely to hand you a needle and thread than a lecture if she saw a hem hanging or a ladder in a stocking.

Without the continual harassment I began to think that maybe
I might indeed have a vocation: it was such a beautiful life. I used
to find a kind of pleasurable pain in my chest when listening to
the organ as the entire school, girls and nuns, sang in four-part
harmony for benediction. It was all so beautiful, the blue and
gold mosaic in the chapel, the tasteful arrangements of lilies in
the urns before the altar, the smell of incense and the plaintive
beauty of the nuns' voices singing Holy Office as we girls left the
chapel. I wanted to stay there forever. It all made me feel so
saintly that I could easily imagine myself contentedly living my
life gliding down the polished corridors with a swish of skirt, a
rattle of beads and a rustle of head-dress. I was sure I could get
used to the early rising and become adept at wielding the butter-
knife. 'A lady always uses the butter-knife, even when dining
alone,' Sister Dominic had told us once, and it had impressed me.
I never told a soul that we did not use a butter-knife at home, in
fact we didn't even have one; sometimes I wondered about my
family.

As part of my religious urge, I decided to apply to join the
Children of Mary. They were the elite of the school, it was from
them that the prefects were chosen. You could only join this
sodality if all the teachers and nuns thought you were suitable.
But even before that you had to earn a blue rosette and go on
probation for six weeks. To my delight I got the rosette and I
swore a solemn oath to myself that I would behave like an angel
for that time, to earn my blue cloak and the blue ribbon with the
silver medal of Our Lady on it. But Mairín nearly jeopardized my
chances again.

It was during Irish class. The room was quiet, with only the
sounds of pens writing and pages turning; Bean Uí Shúilleabháin, our craggy-faced teacher from Kerry, despaired of our
Dubliners' ignorance of Gaelic literature – Irish was not a very
popular subject in our school – but everyone knew that she was
a good teacher and that her notes got people through their
Leaving Certificate Irish exams. Mairín raised the lid of her desk
and rested it on the crown of her head as though she was search-
ing for a book. She nudged me and drew my attention to a
magazine which she had in her desk, opening it at a page with a
full-colour picture of Elvis; he wore a white satin shirt and trous-

ers and a big rhinestone-encrusted belt, his pelvis was thrust forward, his guitar was slung low, and his hair was black and shiny. There was something very exciting about him, I leaned over to get a better look.

Suddenly the lid of Mairín's desk was whipped back and Bean Uí Shúilleabháin stood there looking her grimest. She took the magazine out of Mairín's hand and looked at it. 'So this is what you occupy your minds with.' She held the magazine up for everyone to see.

There were a few repressed giggles.

'In nineteen-sixteen brave men died for you. Yes, for you, Mairín Weldon, and you, Margaret McCabe. They died so that you would be free to enjoy your own heritage, your own language, and your own literature. And what do you do with that hard-won freedom? You waste your time on . . . *Stories of the Stars.*'

It probably wouldn't have gone any farther if there hadn't been a knock on the door. In came our mistress of studies, Sister Gervase, known as Waddles, followed by the Reverend Mother. For a moment we were paralysed at the idea of Reverend Mother seeing Elvis.

'Is there some trouble, Bean Uí Shúilleabháin? Sister Gervase asked as she waddled over.

Reverend Mother, pale, gentle and abstracted-looking, wafted after her.

'It seems that some girls prefer to snigger over this than pay attention to their Irish poetry.'

'May I see that? asked Reverend Mother quietly, holding her hand out for the offending magazine still open at the picture of Elvis. 'Who is this person?' she inquired wonderingly of Sister Gervase.

'Perhaps the owner of this . . . er . . . portrait, might like to inform Reverend Mother,' Sister Gervase said in a voice of acid and splintered glass.

Mairín stood up, shoulders back, and looked levelly at the nuns. 'It's Elvis Presley, Mother,' she said, and blushed.

'What a strange name,' murmured Reverend Mother, 'I expect he is some kind of crooner or film actor.

'He's a rock an' roll singer, Mother.'

'Oh dear, I would fear for that young man's soul,' she said, handing the magazine back to Bean Uí Shúilleabháin and shaking her head sorrowfully. 'He is either very bad or very mad.' She turned her pained gaze on Sister Gervase, obviously expecting her to do something about it.

The younger nun coughed and said that she would deal with us after school, and in the meantime Reverend Mother wanted to talk to us about the forthcoming visit of the Mother General.

Later that afternoon Waddles gave us a blistering talking-to and I knew how the more sensitive Israelites felt when Moses found them with the golden calf. She made everybody in the class clear out their desks and throw out anything which was not strictly needed for classwork. She insisted that Mairín and I each write an essay entitled: 'Music hath charms to soothe the savage Breast', and said that she would take this into consideration when our names came up for the Children of Mary.

I was sure that I wouldn't make it but when the day came I was overjoyed to hear my name called out. I received my medal and ribbon from the hands of Mother General herself. I didn't even mind that she had bad breath. When I had got the ribbon and the danger was over I could even enjoy Mairín's hilarious imitation of Reverend Mother's reaction to Elvis.

'I would fear for that poor boy's soul,' mimicked Mairín, 'he's either very bad or very mad. . . . What a square!'

I wasn't much of an Elvis fan, mostly because I wasn't let listen to pop music programmes on radio, but I had to admit that he did have something. He was so different, so exciting; maybe that's why he reminded me of Alan. Alan was a new boy in our neighbourhood and Mairín never stopped talking about him. Everything about him seemed so different to all the other boys who lived locally. He had been born in England and lived in France, and his father, who was a Protestant, had just died. All the other boys I knew had solid Irish names like Seán and Brian and Patrick, wore brown corduroy trousers and pullovers knitted by their mothers, and had plain short-back-and-sides haircuts. Alan wore black drainpipe trousers and had his fair hair swept back in a greased duck's tail. Every time I saw him I felt my heart lurch and my face go hot. I knew I was in love with him but I didn't want anybody to know, especially Mairín. So I pretended that I was not very interested. Of course I wouldn't dream of speaking to him but I kept hoping that some time he would notice me and start a conversation. That's why, whenever I could, I arranged to go to the local shops at the same time as he did. Alan lived in a house that backed onto ours so, when I came home from school each day, I'd go and stand at my bedroom window, watching to see if he would come out of his house. I noticed that at about the same time nearly every day he left with a shopping bag and disappeared down the side passage. Obviously he was going shopping for his mother. My mother too often needed messages and if I timed it right I could be in Kelly's High Class Grocery at the same time as Alan. On the first occasion I arrived just after him.

'What can I get you today, young man?' asked solid Mr Kelly in his brown shop coat.

'A pound of mixed-fruit jam, a quarter of rashers, a turnover and half a dozen eggs,' said Alan.

I listened enraptured to the foreignness of his voice and stood as close to him as I dared. I even touched his jacket and hoped that he would turn and notice me. But I stared in the other direction in case he might think that I fancied him or, even worse, was chasing him. At least I knew that much, that it was always the boys who did the chasing. I daydreamed of walking along the road; he'd come round the corner and say hello, so I'd say hello in an off-hand kind of way; then he'd say: I've seen you around quite a bit and wondered who you are, I'm Alan, what's your name? So I'd tell him my name and then I'd say . . . well I didn't really know what I'd say then, but it would be something interesting, and he'd ask me to go to the pictures with him. What actually happened whenever I saw him come towards me was that I felt butterflies in my stomach, blushed, put my head down and walked past as though absorbed in inner thoughts. As soon as I was past him I'd look round to watch his back disappear out of my life for another day.

Now that I was in love and didn't know when Alan would ask me out on a date, I took much more interest in those interminable conversations about kissing, which Mairín and the others in my class enjoyed. If Alan did ask me out, what should I do? Should I let him kiss me on the lips or only on the cheek? I thought about him kissing me on the lips, wow, imagine. I used to take my pillow in my arms at night and pretend it was him and he was kissing me gently. Not for very long mind you, because it might be a sin, but sometimes I used to imagine that he was holding me tenderly in his arms and that I laid my head on his chest. After that I wasn't too sure what could happen. I had heard talk of french kissing but I didn't know what it was and I couldn't ask anyone without seeming a right eejit. Everyone else seemed to know.

One day there was nobody supervising our piano practice in the music rooms.

'Let's sneak off to the furnace room and talk,' Mairín said to me.

'But we might get caught,' I replied, always nervous of getting into trouble.

'Don't be silly, Margaret, nobody ever comes in here to check. Come on.'

The furnace room must have been a cellar once, for it only had half-windows showing above ground, and a low-watt bulb kept it dim even when the light was on. At some time it must have been converted into a classroom but now it was a storeroom for old books, copies, boxes of pencils, broken music stands and discarded cello cases. These leaned together at the back of the room near the old furnace like tired old companions. Because the furnace was still lit in very cold weather the room was usually warm so it was a favourite place for pupils to sneak off to. This was the first time I'd ever not been where I should be during class time.

'Have you ever kissed a boy?' Mairín asked me.

'No,' I answered rather defensively. 'Have you?'

'Mmmmmmm,' she said, smiling and looking into the distance.

'You mean you did? What happened, tell us.'

Mairín continued to look dreamily into the distance. 'It was during the holidays when I was staying with my aunty in the country. My cousins took me to a dance and I met this fella, Frankie, and he left me home and kissed me.' She stopped and smiled and looked dazed.

'But you never told me.' I felt quite cheated that such an important thing should have happened and she hadn't discussed it with me.

'I'm telling you now, amn't I.'

'OK, but how did it happen? Did he just suddenly kiss you, or what?'

'Oh no, first he took me in his arms and ran his fingers through my hair, then he kissed me on the forehead and then he french kissed me.'

'What was that like?' I asked, all excited that I might be going to find out at last.

'Well I fainted of course.'

'Fainted? But what made you faint?'

'Oh Margaret! Of course I fainted, sure everybody knows that french kissing makes you faint.'

'Did Frankie faint too?' I had an image of the two of them in a dead faint on the doorstep and thought it might be a bit difficult.

'Don't be stupid, why should Frankie faint? It's only girls who faint from it.'

I had a quick flash of fainting prettily into Alan's arms: he lifted me up and placed me tenderly on a velvet sofa, then he dabbed my forehead with his handkerchief of monogrammed white linen.

As I was contemplating this vision we heard footsteps and the rattle of beads. Without a word we climbed in behind the cello cases and were just settled when the door opened and in came Sister Dominic. I held my breath, petrified that she would discover us, all my old terror of her coming back, but she didn't seem to notice anything. She started pacing up and down the room reading her Office. Up and down she paced, up and down. We breathed very gently and I could feel a cramp starting in my leg. She continued pacing and reading and pacing. I eased my leg silently and slowly, but she still stayed there. A bell rang. Music practice was over and it was time for French with boring old Miss Webster. If we didn't arrive there would be questions and trouble. The nun looked as though she would be there forever; we were just going to have to face her and put up with the consequences. We both seemed to realise this at the same time, so together we stood up from behind the cello cases and knocked over a music stand. She whirled round at the sound of the crash.

'Sorry for disturbing you, Sister,' I mumbled.

She dropped her breviary and screamed.

We didn't wait to find out what happened next. We dashed out of the furnace room and back upstairs to our class, laughing and gasping all the way.

'The look on her face!' snorted Mairín. 'Did you see the look on her face?'

'Most unladylike, Sister, most unladylike,' I added, and the two of us fell against the wall laughing.

Later Mairín entertained the whole class to a dramatisation of the scene and we became heroines for a time. Everybody feared and disliked Sister Dominic and thought the incident a suitable revenge, but I waited and waited in dread of the trouble we might get into. Nothing happened however, and then Sister Dominic was transferred to another convent. We all said that it was because she was afraid of the furnace-room ghost.

But I was still in the dark about french kissing and what exactly I should do with a boy on a date; I'd be leaving school in June and felt that I'd need to know by then. That's why I was looking forward to the long religious retreat which we had at Easter. There was always a special lecture for the school leavers on chastity and marriage when, rumour had it, we would learn all. Already we had some hints from the nuns. 'Young men have passions,' Sister Evangeline, our religious knowledge teacher had hinted darkly, 'passions which once aroused are difficult if not impossible for them to control. You must be careful not to arouse those passions or become an occasion of sin for a boy.' But what exactly were those passions and how could I arouse them? Maybe I was doing it already and didn't know. 'Dress', elucidated Sister Rose during one of her weekly talks, 'can be an occasion of sin. The neck of your dress should never be lower than the width of two fingers from the base of your neck. You could unwittingly cause a man to commit sin by wearing a plunging neckline.' Well there was no fear of that for me, my parents wouldn't let me wear anything which could be considered immodest. They wouldn't even let me wear trousers, never mind plunging necklines. I still thought there must be more to it.

Retreat time came and we sat respectfully through the talks on Our Lady, The Real Presence, Sin and Hell and, at last, Chastity and Marriage. Father O'Callaghan talked a lot about the ideals of Catholic girlhood, the danger of mixed marriage and the need to model ourselves on Our Lady. He said nothing about dates with boys, french kissing or fainting. It was disappointing but question time, in the library, was still to come. Sister Gervase had told us beforehand that we could write down any questions which we would like Father O'Callaghan to answer and put them in a box which she would leave in the library. We sat there waiting for him to come and, although we weren't supposed to talk during the retreat, we whispered to one another with suppressed excitement.

The priest came in at last, closed the door and sat down at the table in front of us. He cleared his throat, smiled encouragingly and said, 'Well now, I believe I'm here to answer any questions, so let's hear them.' He linked his fingers and leaned back in his chair.

There was a deadly silence and we all looked at our shoes. Someone suppressed a hysterical giggle. Eventually somebody in the front row indicated the box on the table.

'Oh I see, all right, let's start with these then.' He drew the box towards him, chose a piece of paper and held it at a distance while he searched for his spectacles. Then he read aloud, 'How far can you go with a boy on a date?' He paused and smiled round the room.

This is it, I thought.

'I suppose it all depends on how much time you have. You could go all round the world, if you liked and had the time and money.' He beamed at us, pleased with his little joke.

We giggled politely in anticipation.

'How far can you go with a boy? I'd say that you could go just as *far* with a boy as I could with Reverend Mother.'

This time we all laughed out loud. The very thought of it, Reverend Mother and Father O'Callaghan out on a date!

'I'm quite serious,' he continued after we had settled down again, 'when you are out with a boy you should do nothing which would be considered improper for me to do with

Reverend Mother. Let's go on to the next question.' He drew out another piece of paper. 'How long should a kiss last?' He smiled. 'Again it depends doesn't it? If you're kissing your mother, how long would you want it to last? However, if you're kissing your boyfriend that's a different matter altogether. You could be in grave danger of committing sin or being an occasion of sin. Always remember that boys look to you as examples of *chastity* and that they have no respect for a girl who leads them into sin.' He took out the next piece of paper and read it. 'I don't think it is appropriate to read this out,' he said, and reached into the box again.

It was probably some question about close dancing, I thought.

The priest talked on and on, warning about occasions of sin and making his little jokes. I was impatient for him to get to my question, but when he read out the last question in the box I realised. Mine must have been the one that was inappropriate to read out. Now I'd never know about french kissing and fainting. Later on, the rest of the class speculated about what the question could have been and who could have written it. I didn't tell a soul, especially not Mairín.

So I left St Saviour's that June after I'd finished the Leaving Certificate Examination. I was well prepared for recognising occasions of sin. I had been warned about the evils of communism. I knew how to answer if an atheist questioned my faith. And, though I had shelved the idea of becoming a nun, I was ready to get myself involved in lay Catholic action as soon as the opportunity arose. I didn't have much idea of what to do with my life.

*   *   *

Eventually Oliver stopped snoring and I dropped off to sleep.

2

NEXT MORNING in St Brigid's, Sister Magdalen was waiting for
me. She had her veiled look. 'Miss McCabe,' she called, and
beckoned with her forefinger – she has a very sinister beckon,
like a Roman Emperor to a Christian he's looking forward to
seeing mauled; when I was a schoolgirl, Sister Dominic, my form
mistress, used to beckon like that too – 'I'd like to have a private
word with you before you go to class. Perhaps somebody could
keep an eye . . .' she spotted Kathy, my friend, on her way to class.
'Miss Ferguson, would you mind keeping an eye on Miss
McCabe's class while I have a little word with her?'

'Yes, of course, Sister.' Kathy slipped behind her with a
what's-going-on expression on her face. She gave me a thumbs
up and Sister Magdalen a fingers up sign, and left. Kathy was not
one of the devoted fans.

Sister Magdalen brought me to her office and closed the door.
'Well, Miss McCabe?' She lifted her shoulders in a huge intake of
breath which she didn't appear to let go. She stood there moving
the things on her desk fractionally, as though she couldn't begin
properly until her papers were all precisely positioned. 'What's
all this I hear about your class, the the, eh, the facts of er, um, of
procreation?'

How did she know about that? She must have been quizzing
the kids. I always suspected she did that, sneaky bitch. 'I'm not
sure what you want to know, Sister,' I replied, injecting the
maximum insolence into my tone of voice as I stalled for time.

'Is it true that you told your class the facts of, er, human reproduction?'

'Well yes, of course.'

'Why of course?'

'Well, the question arose and it seemed like a good opportunity.' I explained the circumstances.

'Was that on your programme of lessons for the week?'

'No, Sister, it wasn't. But as you know, you have to be flexible with these children. You cannot always stick to strict prorammes.'

She flushed at that and pursed her lips slightly. She could recognise her own words being used against her. She did not like it: it smelled of sedition. 'Of course, Miss McCabe, of course. But you know, there are some matters that are very delicate and we do have to be particularly careful with our children. After all, human reproduction is not merely a question of facts, there is also the question of morality to be considered.' She paused.

I kept the blankest expression I could on my face. I thought of my eyes as pools-of-nothingness, like a reactivated Frankenstein corpse.

She smiled patiently and continued, 'Perhaps you have forgotten that the school policy is that such information should be given individually to each child and in a religious context.' She paused between each sentence as though I were rather slow and needed time to absorb each piece of information. 'I'd like to see each one of the children in your class today. Send them down to me, one by one. I'll speak to each of them myself.' Her tone of voice left me in no doubt that this extra task she now had was entirely my fault.

'But Sister,' I protested, 'there's no need for you to see them, I think they have all the information they need.'

'And what about the religious aspects?'

'Religious aspects, well, I . . .' I searched around for a suitable remark.

'Surely, Miss McCabe, you are aware of the recommendation made by His Grace, the Archbishop, in his Pastoral Letter?'

'Mmmmmmm.' I tried to look as though I read a page of it every day before breakfast.

'You must remember his advice that the sacred and delicate task of transmitting information about procreation should be taken on by the parents, and where this is not possible it should be done individually and within the religious context. He does not consider it appropriate to give that information to an entire class.

I tried hard to keep my pools-of-nothingness expression. I felt the muscles in my jaw tightening with anger and frustration. I knew I had done the right thing, it would have been silly to avoid Pat's question, and here was this woman trying to make me feel like a criminal or something. But I didn't say anything, there was no point: if I argued with her she'd only ask me if I were feeling well and whether I shouldn't see a doctor.

'Send the girls down to me, one by one.' She sighed.

Silly cow, I thought.

She was already speaking charmingly into the telephone.

I walked up to my classroom, fuming. What kind of an eejit is she at all? Where on earth does she think those kids come from anyway? Doesn't she know their brothers are in jail for robbery with violence, their sisters are on the game? They'll probably all get pregnant long before they get married, while they're still in their early or middle teens. If they're to have any chance of changing the pattern they need clear unequivocal information. Pious pamphlets about love and respect and the sanctity of matrimony are not going to be of any use.

Mary Haverty was only swaying gently, so things must have been all right in the class. The minute I got in the door Pearl jumped up from her place and said, 'Miss, oh miss, what about twins?' 'And triplets, please, miss,' Angela added. Next thing a babble broke out. They all seemed to have questions. 'Hang on girls, give me a chance to get in the door,' I said, as I went to my desk. 'Now tell me what's the problem?'

It seemed that a discussion about the cause of multiple births had started and the arguments were almost turning into rows. I could hardly go all coy on them and say that my lips were sealed, that Sister Magdalen would answer all further questions. They'd think I was gone cracked. Besides, I wasn't going to mess up the trust they had in me. Well, to hell with Sister Magdalen! I told them all about twins, triplets, quads, quins and fertility drugs, with diagrams.

The door opened suddenly, no knock, nothing, and Sister Magdalen walked in. 'Miss McCabe,' she acknowledged me with a slight inclination of her head, and without asking my permission continued, 'I'd like to speak privately with each of you girls.'

Oh my God, I'd forgotten to send them down, in the fuss. Talk about a Freudian slip!

'Now, who'd like to come first?'

There was dead silence. Nobody was anxious to be closeted with the Principal.

'I suppose it depends on what you are doing just now.' She smiled charmingly at me, and looked at the blackboard. Her smile spoiled rather when she flared her nostrils.

'We were just going over last night's homework, Sister,' piped up Pat, lying with conviction.

'Mmmm, I see, well Angela, perhaps you had better come first. When you come back you can send down Michele, and then Pearl, and so on. Is that clear, Miss McCabe?'

'Perfectly, Sister.'

She left with Angela, who was looking nervous.

'Fuckin' penguin,' hissed Pat, almost before the door was closed.

'Now, Pat, that's enough.'

'But, miss, she is. They're all the same, nuns, sneaky fuckin' penguins.'

'Patricia, that is quite enough.'

'But miss, she was at us last night to know what you are teaching us, an' Andrea told her about the babies an' I told her she shouldn't have.'

So, it was true. She did quiz the children about class. Patricia was right. I decided I'd better change the subject fast. 'Now everybody, back to your desks, I'm going to tell you a story.' They loved stories. It was one way of getting them down to their English lesson.

In the middle of the story Angela came back, looking worried, and Michele went down to Sister Magdalen's office. And so the morning wore on.

At lunchtime Kathy wanted to know what The Mag, as we called the Principal, had wanted me for. We were waiting in the staffroom for the kettle to boil. Nora Harvey and Geraldine Byrne joined us. I gave them a blow by blow account of what had happened. 'Typical!' said Kathy. 'What else would you expect?'

added Nora. 'She really has no right to walk into your classroom like that without knocking. You shouldn't put up with it,' said Geraldine, who was very hot on rights, and what not to put up with. It was nice to know they were all on my side.

Mary was rocking like mad when I got back to my classroom. Angela was chewing the inside of her lip. There was an air of discomfort around.

'Please, miss,' burst out little Natasha Murphy, 'which of youse is right?'

'I'm afraid I don't know what you're talking about, Natasha. Could you explain a bit better?'

'It's Sister Magdalen, miss, that's what she wanted us for this morning, to explain about babies. But she told us we were not allowed to tell anybody at all, and it was different to what you said, miss.'

I groaned inwardly. What on earth had she told them? 'How do you mean, different, Natasha?'

'She told us it was about Christmas – '

'No, no,' interrupted Pearl, 'she started with the Angel Gabriel.'

'And the Holy Ghost.'

'And she told me about the "Hail Mary",' added another.

God, no wonder the poor kids were confused. She chooses the exception to the rule to explain the norm. I did my best to suggest that really Sister Magdalen and I were telling them the same thing, it was just that she wanted to expand their knowledge. I knew by their faces that they didn't really believe me.

On my way home that evening The Mag was waiting for me outside her office. 'Miss McCabe, a moment,' she called, with a saccharin voice and a lemony smile, 'what was the delay in sending the girls to me this morning?'

'I'm sorry, Sister, but it just slipped my mind,' I said, sounding very sincere, 'there was a bit of a fuss when I went into the class. It had to be dealt with immediately.'

'Did our discussion about the communication of facts associated with procreation also slip your mind? I noticed your blackboard this morning.'

'Oh no, Sister, that was there from yesterday,' I lied. 'Excuse me, I have to hurry now as I have an appointment.' And I rushed off before she had time to say anything else.

'She can't even say the word sex!' I exploded to Kathy on the way home. 'She has to think of long phrases.'

'Really, the way that woman behaves!' Kathy shook her head in despair, 'You'd think we were all bold little schoolgirls. We really shouldn't put up with it.'

'I suppose we shouldn't, but I've had enough hassle with her over the Union. I'll take the easy way out now.'

'Yes, I suppose you're right. She'd only make your life a complete misery if you dared to disagree with her.'

For the rest of the afternoon I argued in my head with Sister Magdalen. I thought of at least eight different devastating replies, but I knew I'd never really have the nerve to say them. I continued complaining and arguing about Sister Magdalen in my head till Oliver came home that evening.

He started preparing dinner. It was his main claim to being liberated, the fact that he did a lot of the cooking. When I cook, I abandon the recipes and add a little of this and a dash of that. He thinks that's inexact, unscientific and typical of women. When he cooks everything has to be exact to the milligram, you'd think he was discovering the cure for cancer.

'Have a good day?' he asked as he adjusted the cooker flame by a hair's breadth.

'Oh my God, Oliver, I've had a terrible day – '

'So have I,' he interrupted before I could say any more. 'Every single thing which could go wrong went wrong. That eejit Johnny O'Loughlin came in late again and hung-over too. He really has a drink problem that guy. I'm going to have to get rid of him if he goes on like this.'

I listened to a long saga of woes and thought that I'd wait till he was finished and then he could listen to me. There was no point in talking to him now, he was too preoccupied. But I did want to tell him about my troubles. I needed the sympathy.

'I had this ridiculous row with Sister Magdalen today,' I began when we had finished eating and Oliver seemed in good humour.

He got up and went out to the kitchen.

I sighed. 'Oliver, I do wish you'd listen to me sometimes.'

'I am listening, where did you put the toothpicks?'

I didn't answer, just waited for him to come back, and fumed.

'It was about sex instruction. You should have heard what she told them – '

'Nuns are all frustrated. I'm not surprised,' he interrupted, and glanced at the television page in the evening paper.

'Oh, Oliver, it's all very well for you to say that, but you don't know what she's like to work for,' I wailed.

'You're far too sensitive, Margaret. That's your problem. You'd have to toughen up if you were in business like me.'

'Oliver, you don't understand, she treats us all like little girls.'

'Well, why don't you leave then?'

'It's not that easy, and I do really like the work with the children.'

But by then he had got up and gone in to turn on the television. Oh it was no use talking to him, he just did not listen. I cleared off the table, did the washing up and wondered what had gone wrong with my life. I had thought that when I left home, got away from the restrictions of living with my parents and came to live with Oliver, that things would be different. I thought that I'd be liberated or something.

Liberated, me Granny!

Oliver went to bed and left me to mull over my life.

*   *   *

Mairín wasn't with me on my first day in UCD and I felt a bit lost. She had announced that she did not want to study any more, that she was going to do shorthand and typing and get a job and money as soon as possible. Her parents were disappointed but they decided that they would only be wasting their money by insisting that she study when she obviously didn't want to.

I found my way to the ladies reading room in the hope of meeting somebody I knew. Nobody from my class would be there but there might just be somebody I'd met before. The room, with a large, creaking mahogany table in the centre had a tattered look. The sagging armchairs round the walls were filled with groups of girls chatting and smoking. I couldn't see anybody I knew. I went over to the mantlepiece with the large mirror over it, to comb my hair and put on the lipstick which my parents wouldn't approve of if they knew about it. At least it was something to do. I was joined by two girls who looked more like models than students. They wore expensive-looking skirts and

V-necked pullovers. Their handbags and shoes matched and their hair looked full and glossy. I felt drab and awkward and embarrassingly unsophisticated. One of the girls took out a tweezers and searched her eyebrows for sign of a superfluous hair; the other took out a little black block of mascara, spat on it and started to apply it to her eyelashes with a tiny brush.

'Do you know how to make your voice sexy?' asked the mascara one.

'No, tell, tell,' enthused the other.

'I was told this by an actress I met during the summer,' said the first, taking out her handkerchief to wipe the smudge she'd made with the mascara. 'First you say, Hello darling, in your normal tone of voice.'

'Hello darling,' said the two of them together.

'Then you change your speaking tone into a singing tone, like this, Hello darling . . . doh, then you sing down the octave, doh tee lah soh fa me re doh. And you change it back again into your speaking tone, only now its much lower and sexier. Hello darling,' she finished in her new sexier voice, raising her eyebrow and looking seductively over her shoulder at her reflection in the mirror.

I must learn how to do that, I thought, feeling a whole new world of devastating sophistication open before me and realising that I had an awful lot to learn. I made my way down to the main hall, thinking about it. The hall was filled with young men in duffle coats, talking and laughing and staring over their shoulders whenever a group of girls passed. I felt too shy to walk through with all those boys looking at me, never mind trying out my Hello darling routine. I went back to the ladies reading room and saw Kathy Ferguson reading the noticeboard.

We greeted one another like old friends although we had only met once before at an inter-schools debate. She had captained the opposing team and, over the jam buns and tea which followed, I had chatted to her. I had liked her then and was overjoyed to meet her now. She had shoulder-length fair hair and what she used to call piebald eyes. If you looked closely you could see that her eyes were different colours. One was hazel and the other had large, golden-brown flecks in it. Although she complained about them, she secretly liked her eyes because they made her look very interesting. 'And anyway, I'm never stuck for something to talk about!' she used to laugh. But the most remarkable thing about Kathy was her sense of adventure. Doing things with her was like being the Famous Five or the Secret Seven, except of course that there were only the two of us. When Kathy and I were together I found it easier to overcome my shyness and chat to people I didn't know over cups of coffee in the Annex, to explore the college societies and get to know who was who.

Kathy had had a very similar education to me so we were both agreed that we should become involved in some kind of lay Catholic action. The Legion of Mary was an obvious choice. The work which the university praesidium of the Legion did was called hall contact. It was a bit of a joke amongst some at least of the members. We were supposed to sit for an hour a week in the main hall of the college and talk to people about the practice of their religion. Naive and all as I was, I knew that it was not really on to stop university students on their way to lectures and ask them if they had been to mass last Sunday and when they had last been to confession. So Kathy and I compromised by doing our hour a week in the main hall and using the time to chat to anybody who chanced along. It was a great way of getting to know people and, being Ireland, the subject of religion inevitably came up, so we felt that we were keeping within the spirit of the Legion work. I was quite surprised to learn how many of the people I met were very critical of the Church, of priests, of nuns and of the monopoly the Church has on the educational system. I found as I listened that I agreed with a lot of what I heard, but nothing seriously challenged my faith until the day Eamonn Butler came along.

He was a first year like myself, but quite unlike the rest of us in the class. For a start he was quite old, twenty-five at least, and he had worked before he came to college. He was tall and handsome and I had overheard somebody in the ladies reading room describe him as byronic. I assumed she was referring to his mane of thick dark curly hair. During tutorials he was always asking questions which I didn't really understand and quoting from books I'd never heard of. But the most fascinating thing about him was the rumour that he had lost his job because he was an atheist; they said that he had refused to teach religion in the national school where he'd worked, so the parish priest who was his employer fired him. I had always pictured atheists as squat, adenoidal types who lived in London, wrote in Communist newspapers and plotted against the Catholic Church. I had never expected to meet any of them here in Ireland where everyone was Catholic. Well not everyone, but at least we all had some religion.

One afternoon while Kathy and I were sitting in the hall doing our Legion work, Eamonn came down the stairs from the lecture theatres and joined us.

'What are the two of you up to this cold afternoon?' he asked.

'We're doing our Legion work.' Kathy smiled, flicking back her fair hair. I wished I had put on some lipstick because, whatever about being an atheist, he was very handsome.

'My God, the Legion,' he declared, 'this is no afternoon for Legion work, it is a time for returning to the womb.'

I had no idea what he was talking about but I was at a stage where I was deeply impressed by anything I didn't understand. He had a deep resonant voice and a soft western accent which gave his words a greater significance than if they had been said by anybody else.

'Wouldn't you agree,' he continued, 'that February is a time for hibernation, a time for regeneration, a time for restoration, a time to creep back through time and space into the warm, wet, comforting darkness of the womb?'

I was quite disconcerted by this, I was not used to discussing wombs in mixed company. At the same time I didn't want to appear silly and shockable and to be labelled a convent bunny, so I nodded and frowned and tried to look intellectual.

'Did you know,' Eamonn continued, 'that the founder of the Legion of Mary, Frank Duff, modelled his organisation on the Roman army?'

'Yes of course,' I replied casually, glad to be on safe ground again.

'So you are both soldiers of Christ then?'

'Well, we're members of the Legion anyway,' I replied.

'And you don't mind the militaristic implications?'

I didn't know if he was mocking us or not. He seemed quite serious.

'We feel that the laity should be involved in the work of the

Church,' Kathy said, and I nodded in agreement with her, 'and this is what we have decided is our contribution.'

Maybe our example might make him think, maybe even convert him.

'Religion is the opium of the people,' said Eamonn, and he shook his head sadly as though contemplating in pity the great numbers of the drugged.

Of course I didn't agree with him, but I was struck by the originality of his phrase, which I assumed was his own.

'Does God exist or is God dead?' he asked of the air, and continued on to answer himself in a complex argument.

I wasn't sure I followed the finer points but I was sure of one thing, that I knew the five proofs of the existence of God. I had learned them from the *Apologetics of Catholic Teaching* which we had in school and which we had been told would prove invaluable whenever we were challenged about our religion or questioned about our faith. I began to quote them to Eamonn; I knew them off by heart, so did Kathy, and she joined in enthusiastically.

Eamonn listened with flattering attention. 'Mmmmm,' he said when we had finished, 'so they're still teaching you those tired old arguments.'

'How do you mean?' I asked, a bit taken aback.

'Let me tell you girls, it's about time you knew that no matter what the nuns taught you in school, those arguments are not conclusive. Obviously, if they were, anybody of any intelligence would bow to their logic, wouldn't they?'

'I suppose so,' I agreed cautiously.

'But my dears, there are innumerable men of magnificent intelligence who cannot accept the existence of a supreme being and they are being justified by the scientific discoveries which prove that all life stems from some cosmic disaster and not from the Garden of Eden.'

I'd never thought about that before and neither had Kathy. It did make some kind of sense. We talked about it for a long time after Eamonn had gone. Shortly afterwards we decided to abandon the Legion of Mary because we were developing doubts.

Of course anybody who had the faintest pretensions to being

thought intellectual had doubts about the Church. It went hand in hand with reading banned books and dismissing as simplistic the view of history which we had been taught in school. We talked about it in the Annex over cups of coffee and tipsey cakes, over well-nursed pints in O'Dwyers public house and in debates at the Literary and Historical Society on a Saturday night. I began to feel that at last I was really learning something about life and toyed with calling myself an agnostic.

At home I argued with my father about papal infallibility and the Censorship Board. He threw up his hands to heaven and begged God to tell him why on earth he had sent me to university when all I was learning was to be a pagan. But I still went dutifully to mass, although I drew the line at benediction, the Women's Sodality and the May devotions.

It was close to examination time at the end of my first year and I was feeling a bit frantic. I had spent a lot of time discussing life and very little in the library so now I had to make up for lost time.

'The May procession is on next Sunday,' my mother announced after supper one evening.

Neither Patrick nor I said a word. Lucy wasn't there because she had married recently. The Boring Barrister was what Patrick and I called her husband.

'I'm speaking to the two of you,' my mother said, 'I expect both of you to be there.'

'Not me, Mam,' said Patrick, looking up briefly from the magazine he was reading. 'I'll be away climbing.' He put a foot up on a vacant chair and continued reading.

'It's only one weekend in the year,' interjected my father, 'surely that's not too much to ask of you, to give up one weekend to Our lady. It wouldn't exactly kill you.'

'I have this arranged for some time,' answered Patrick without looking up.

'Look at me when you speak and take your feet off the chair.'

'OK, OK, relax, take it easy,' said Patrick, taking his foot down and rising to leave the room.

'Pagan!' shouted my father after him.

Patrick was in his final year of architecture and could get away with anything he liked, not so me.

'You'll be there won't you, Margaret?' asked my mother.

'Ma, I do have exams you know and I'll have to study.'

'If your examinations are depending on the little bit of knowledge you could get into your head during the May procession, well there's not much hope for you,' said my father testily.

'Don't you think Our Lady would help you with your examinations, Margaret? Especially as you are a Child of Mary and will be at the top of the procession. Our Lady always looks after her own.'

Maybe she was right. I was superstitious about examinations. Maybe if I didn't go I'd fail, there might be no harm in having a bit of divine intervention. But I didn't want to walk with the Children of Mary. It was all very well in school but in our local parish church the only people to wear the blue cloak and veil were doddering and diseased inmates of the local old people's home and a few pius ladies whom Patrick called the Holy Water Hens.

'I think I'll just join in with the ordinary people,' I said.

'For the May procession!' exclaimed my mother. 'For the month of Our Lady! Surely you're not ashamed to be counted amongst her children. Get me your cloak and veil and I'll iron them for you.'

I wished that I had Patrick's nerve to refuse. Instead I just gave in.

The day of the procession was brilliantly sunny so there was no chance that it would be cancelled. I left the house as late as I could and slipped into the back of the church. The organist played *con brio* and sang lustily in the loft. He had a soaring tenor voice and pitched everything to suit his range. It meant that the singing was very poor because nobody could keep up with him; even Father Fagin, the parish priest, noted for his fine voice, found it difficult to sing along an octave lower. The priest came down the aisle in his gold cope. He was flanked by two red-soutaned altar boys swinging thuribles and followed by all the rest of the altarboys. Some of the smaller ones were almost turning over on their ankles with the strain of walking so slowly. Then came the statue of Our Lady surrounded with flowers. It was standing inside a plywood conveyance with crude fretwork sides, painted cream and blue with gold bits round the edges; it looked like something that should have been on the back of an elephant, but instead it was carried by the men who passed round the collection plates on a Sunday. My father was one of them. They wore their best suits and looked very serious and responsible. Next came the First Communicants, little girls in frothy white veils and dresses and little boys in severe dark, short-trousered suits and sporting big white rosettes. Then the dreaded Children of Mary shambled past. I was furious with my mother for insisting that I walk with them: they were all old and dowdy and mumbled over prayer-books stuffed with holy pictures and novena leaflets and had rosary beads dripping with medals.

I waited till I saw little Miss Farrelly – Patrick and I used to call her Larks Legs because of the way she walked with her legs sticking out – strutting down the church, her blue cloak billowing behind her and her hands clutching beads under her bosom; on her thin little legs she looked uncommonly like some unusual bird. She was a pleasant, chatty little woman who spent a lot of time going on pilgrimages from which she brought back leaflets and medals, but I knew that she would surely break the monotony of the procession by talking to me. I slipped in beside her. Waddling, wheezey old Miss McGinnity, the parish priest's housekeeper, joined us. At the start of the first Joyful Mystery of the Rosary we moved past the garda on point duty outside the church: his right hand was raised in a salute to the procession and his left held back the traffic while we passed. By the third Joyful Mystery we were passing by our house – most of the houses along the route were decorated, some had bunting, some Papal or Irish flags and yet others had altars to Our Lady in the windows, our house had everything – I looked at it and felt embarrassed by the display. But at least it was done with some taste, that was my mother's doing.

'Your mammy has the house gorgeous, hasn't she, Margaret,' murmured Miss Farrelly to me. 'My sister Sadie was just saying it to me the other day. "Dear," she said, "doesn't Mrs McCabe always do up the house beautifully for the procession." That's what she said.'

Miss McGinnity, on the other side, belched and excused herself. 'I said the same to Father Fagin only yesterday.' She liked to think of herself as the parish priest's plenipotentiary holding sway over the clerk of the church, the teachers in the parish school, leaders of the sodalities, members of the Altar Society and even the curates themselves. Access to the PP was strictly through Miss McGinnity. She farted. I distinctly heard her. 'Oh excuse me, it's the wind,' she wheezed into a handkerchief, 'the wind and the chest, I'm a martyr to them both.'

'My sister Sadie and me are going on a pilgrimage to Loretto in September.' Miss Farrelly obviously didn't wish to hear more of Miss McGinnity's ailments. 'Have you ever heard of the miracle of the flying house of Loretto?'

Before I could answer a hymn had started and Miss Farrelly joined in, her voice thin and reedy and a little off-key.

'Flatulence and the bronichals, that's what the doctore calls it. He tells me there's no cure. Father Fagin says I'll get my reward in the next life because I've had my purgatory in this.'

Belching her way to heaven, I thought, farting to paradise. I grinned to myself and thought that I must remember to tell Patrick later. In fact I felt rather embarrassed by Miss McGinnity's frankness about her condition, but I thought it could make a very funny story.

The roundabout on the Dunmore Road was the half-way mark. An altar had been built there. Slowly the road around the patch of green began to fill up: the First Communicants, the Children of Mary, the Women's Sodality, the Men's Sodality, the Youth Sodality and at last all the ordinary parishioners. We all stood there answering Father Fagin's Hail Mary's. Two dogs were playing on the grass. One of the stewards chased them away. The rosary continued. A First Communicant got sick and had to be taken to a nearby house. Somebody had to locate her mother in the Women's Sodality. Someone else fainted. The stewards were too busy to notice that the dogs were back again playing on the grass. Suddenly I realised that they were not playing, they were – a number of phrases jumped into my mind – committing adultery, fornicating, doing it. Yes they were doing it right there in front of everybody. In front of the parish priest, the Women's Sodality, my parents! I didn't know where to look and I couldn't keep my eyes off them. Some of the boys in the Youth Sodality had their hands over their faces and their heads down. Most people looked straight ahead and answered the prayers as though nothing was happening. There were some people who were so concentrated on the rosary that they didn't notice, but Miss McGinnity was not one of them.

'Those animals have no respect,' she said, quite loud. 'Wouldn't you think that they'd have the decency to wait till night time, or at least till the procession is over.'

The parish priest started another hymn through his mega-phone. 'Immaculate, Im-mac-ul-ate,' sang Miss McGinnity, joining in with her employer.

I noticed a few people hiding smiles. At last it all fitted together for me. All the bits of information and misinformation I had heard over the years, all the dirty jokes and the oblique refer-ences. I remembered the boy I met at a party who tried to maul me all over; I remembered that although I didn't let him I did want him to. Now I knew where it all led to. Now I knew exactly how one got pregnant.

By the time I left university I had discovered that most boys wanted to get inside your clothes but, because they had been brought up in good Irish Catholic schools, they also knew that what they were doing was a sin so they were fairly easy to control. What the nuns had not told me was that I might have passions too. Despite my doubts about religion and the liberal attitudes I liked to strike in conversation with my friends, the fear of mortal sin and pregnancy kept my passions under control.

Apart from learning about sex while I was in college I also learned to discuss obscure continental films with the best of them. I read lots and lots of books I didn't enjoy much, but that very fact proved how good they were. I developed a general and not very well-thought-out tendency to support the underdog, which I liked to think made me a socialist. My father however was convinced that I was in the pay of the Kremlin. But I still didn't have any clear idea what I wanted to do with my life. I didn't want to marry a boring old Bernard, as Lucy had, that's all I was sure of. Anyway I had an arts degree, so I supposed that meant I would teach. And besides, the holidays would be long.

I had no difficulty in getting a job in Mount Olivet, an expensive, well-run secondary school for the daughters of the professional classes. The Sisters of Mount Olivet had all been educated at French finishing schools and had exquisite manners. They expected a high academic standard because the barristers and surgeons who paid them their large school fees wanted only the best. Most of the girls were expected to go to university. The lay staff were very depressing: half of them were elderly, wore severe tweeds and tight-necked blouses, and held definitive views on everything; the rest were fluttery and harassed-looking.

The first day I was there I came into the staff room, smiled engagingly all round, made some amiable comment about the weather and sat down. Nobody took much notice of me until Miss Quinn, one of the tweed skirt types, who was all angular bones, came over. 'Do you mind?' she said, with a tightening of the lips which might well have been a smile. 'Sorry, what?' I said, looking up from *The Irish Times*, not too sure what she was talking about. 'My chair,' she said, with another slight mouth widening. 'Oh, I am sorry,' I scrambled up, knocking over my handbag, which spilled out an embarrassing collection of soiled tissues. Miss Quinn took a deep breath and allowed it out slowly through quivering nostrils as though I were an awkward second year. Each of the armchairs, it turned out, 'belonged' to one or other of the teachers. As I was the most junior member of staff I had to be satisfied with one of the tubular steel chairs.

Later in the same week I had the misfortune to pour tea into the nearest cup at lunchtime. Mrs Logan, who taught Irish and German, leaned over and, taking the cup, said determinedly, 'Excuse me, I'm afraid you are using my cup.' She brought it over to the sink, threw out the tea and washed it carefully. Then she poured some more tea for herself. 'Oh, I'm sorry. I didn't know,' I mumbled, wondering how I could have so polluted her cup that she felt she had to wash it. I hadn't even touched it, just poured the tea. After lunch I saw her wrap her cup in muslin before returning it to the cupboard.

Next I made a *faux-pas* with Mrs Murnaghan, the Classics teacher. The first time I sat near her in the staff room I got an overpowering smell of Polo Mints. 'Come on, own up,' I exclaimed gaily, as though I were with my college friends, 'who has the mints? I'm dying for one.' There was a distinct lowering of the room temperature as eyes shifted and lips pursed. Mrs Murnaghan went red, dropped some copy books and mumbled, 'Yes, of course, certainly, yes, just a moment,' and dived headlong into her huge leather bag. It was then I got a glimpse of the whiskey bottle which she carried round with her. It explained the reason for the mints. 'Oh, no. I was only joking. I mean, it's all right. I didn't . . .' I stumbled. She insisted, and I had to eat it under the disapproving looks of the rest of the staff.

I never really felt accepted amongst the staff. I was replacing old Sister Agidia, who had retired. 'A brilliant mind, you know,' Miss Quinn constantly reminded me, 'Sister Agidia was a truly inspired teacher and a woman of immense wisdom.' I didn't think I could live up to that standard. Oh, how I missed college and the long discussions we used to have. These teachers never talked about anything except school and when the next increment was due. I consoled myself with the thought of the holidays.

One of the things I wanted the long holidays for was travel. Kathy, who was teaching also, and I planned to set off for Europe the instant we got our summer break. We had no firm idea where we'd go. We'd just take our rucksacks and wander south to the sun and adventure.

The evening of the day when the school closed my parents drove me out to Dun Laoghaire to get the boat to Holyhead. Kathy's parents, too, had come to see us off. Our fathers looked pleased and our mothers looked worried.

'Isn't it well for these young ones nowadays!' Mr Ferguson said to my father. 'Off to the Continent, no less!'

'Indeed, indeed,' Daddy agreed, 'out baling hay in the fields was all the holidays we ever got. Isn't that so?'

They smiled and stood back and watched indulgently while our mothers fussed. Kathy and I got into a tizzy of excitement, checking once again that we had our money, our passports and our tickets. My mother took a small plastic bottle out of her handbag. 'Here's some holy water to take with you,' she said confidentially, and slipped it into a side pocket of my rucksack. 'Have you got your missal?'

'Yes, sure I have,' I replied impatiently. I had no intention of travelling round Europe with a missal, but I didn't want her to start getting into a fever. If I told her she'd think it meant that I wouldn't go to mass.

The first shock of travel was the naked girls in London. We stayed in a youth hostel run by a no-nonsense, middle-aged couple who couldn't have been anything but English – they conjured an image of baggy shorts and jolly tramps across the moors – but that's where the Englishness of the hostel stopped; London in mid-June was full of the young of Europe, there to see swinging Carnaby Street. The girls in our dormitory were tall Scandinavians and Germans, laughing and talking incomprehensibly to one another. Going to bed that first night, Kathy and I wrestled modestly with our underwear under the cover of our nighties. As I lay in my bunk waiting for the lights to be turned off, I realised that most of the other girls made no attempt to cover themselves. The tall blondes stripped unselfconsciously, and even stopped to talk to one another without a stitch on. I was fascinated and rather shocked, and found myself staring at those lean, sun-tanned bodies. A devastatingly beautiful German girl, wearing only her briefs, was rummaging in her rucksack. She looked up and caught my eye and smiled. I turned away quickly, closing my eyes, ashamed of being caught staring. In the morning, getting dressed, I felt even more self-conscious about exposing any part of my pale body.

'What did you think of the naked ladies?' asked Kathy when we had left the hostel to see the sights.

'Oh, that wouldn't bother me,' I replied dismissively.

'Me neither. I was just thinking about Sister Immaculata in school. She'd have a fit. When we were boarders it was considered immodest to walk down the dormitory in a nightdress without a dressing gown.'

'We were taught so much rubbish in school,' I said.

We both smiled and felt pleased that we'd grown beyond that stage. But I still felt mortally embarrassed at having to take off my bra in the middle of a dormitory full of strangers.

After three days of sightseeing in London we took the train non-stop through France. The French were just as rude to us as Uncle Billy and Aunty Joan, who had been in Lourdes for the Marian Year, had warned us they would be. Nobody bothered to take any trouble to understand my Leaving Certificate (honours) French, which made it really difficult to get information. Once we crossed the border into Spain everything changed. Our train was taken over by a great horde of people from another train. Small, dark, wiry men pushed their cardboard suitcases through the windows, a garrulous crone with a deeply lined face and a black headscarf was hooshed up the steps into our carriage, women with dyed hair and pasty-faced babies climbed aboard. In no time at all we were surrounded with shouts and talk and gestures: Spaniards returning home after their year's work in Germany.

They told us about the huge amounts of money they could earn in Frankfurt, and the hard work. As soon as the train moved out of the station and the first windowfulls of Spain could be seen, they raised a cheer and started to sing.

Kathy and I were beside ourselves with delight. The smell of garlic, the noise, the discomfort only seemed to make the experience more real. The old woman in the corner ruled our carriage. She demanded to know where we were from.

'Irlanda,' replied Kathy.

'Hollanda?' she said wonderingly.

'Windmills, tulips,' gestured one of the men.

'No, no, Ir-lan-da.'

'Ah, sí, sí, sí, Islandia,' persisted the man, 'eskimo, igloo.'

'No, no, no,' interrupted another man, 'Irlanda, De Valera.' He nodded at us for confirmation.

'Sí, sí,' we chorused triumphantly.

A burst of Spanish broke out, and everybody told everybody else where we were from. Every so often someone would smile and say, 'Irlanda, De Valera,' to us.

'Viva la revolución!' said one.

'What's going on?' I asked Kathy.

'I don't really know. They're talking too fast for me and they're speaking in a dialect, I think, but as far as I can make out, the guy who mentioned De Valera seems to be telling them about the Easter Rising and 1916.'

'Irlanda, boom, boom, Inglaterra, bueno, bueno,' said one of the men to us with appropriate gestures, confirming Kathy's guess.

Whatever version of Irish history they were getting seemed to please them greatly but I suspected from their expressions that they hadn't too much of a clue where Ireland was.

The old lady in the corner unrolled a large lumpy parcel wrapped in cloth and took out a hard dark sausage. She cut lumps off it with a penknife and handed them to us. It seemed to be a sign to the others to take out boxes and bottles. Soon we were being offered more cheese, bread, sausage and wine than we could handle. We ate as much as we could, because we didn't want to offend our new friends. The people in our carriage, we learned, were part of a large group going to Valencia. News of our presence soon spread to friends and cousins down the train, so that by the time we got off in Barcelona we got a noisy farewell.

'Viva Valencia!' someone shouted as we stood waving on the platform. 'Viva!' yelled the crowd on the train, and we joined in as loudly as the rest. 'Viva Irlanda! Viva De Valera!' shouted a man from our carriage. 'Viva, viva!' the crowd roared back. 'Viva España!' screamed the old lady, as the train began to move. 'Viva, viva, viva! the entire train screamed back. I knew I was going to love Spain.

The youth hostel in Barcelona was a primary school temporarily converted for the summer. The warden, a crippled gnome who sat in a dingy little office with a permanently lit yellow bulb hanging from a frayed flex, had a tattered shoe box where he kept our hostel cards. It made up for its lack of facilities by its disregard for international hostelling rules: we could drink wine with our meals and stay out as late as we liked. Kathy and I couldn't ask for better. Together, we explored the city, amazed and delighted by the sun, the colour, and the fact that it never, ever rained.

Then we hitch-hiked from Barcelona to Madrid. The first driver we met wanted us to go to a hotel with him. We refused politely.

'For half an hour only,' he pleaded.

'No, no. We need to get to Madrid,' we replied.

'But I die of love for you. You must come with me.'

'No, thank you. No,' we insisted, beginning to worry that he might kidnap us.

He continued to exclaim and declare passion for us, and

eventually got annoyed and flung his wallet at us. 'Take all my money. Take my car. Take everything, but please, come to the hotel,' he begged.

At that point we drew ourselves up, full of dignity, and Kathy told him in Spanish that she was not that kind of girl and that neither was I. At last he let us out of his car. Safe on the side of the road again, we fell around laughing, partly in relief, partly at his extravagant declarations, and partly at the thrill of adventure.

In Spain, as in London, we tried to see everything we had ever heard of, the Prado, the Alhambra, the gypsy dancers, the Escorial. Eventually we arrived in Malaga reeling with culture, and agreed that a rest by the sea would be a good idea. We took a rattling bus along the coast and stopped in a small fishing village which was doing its best to turn into a tourist resort. As yet the tourists who were in Las Arenas were the kind who go to places where there aren't many tourists. We lay on the beach and got badly sunburnt. Our delicate Celtic skin turned bright red and peeled prodigiously, but that didn't seem to deter the Spanish men. 'Ay que guapa!' they called to us in the street, and Kathy told me it meant 'How beautiful'.

On our second day we met Jesus and Pedro. As we lay on the bright beach, stunned with the sun and the light, a ball bounced beside us, spraying us with sand. Two young men came over and started to apologise profusely. We smiled a recognition of their apology and went back to being stunned. They persisted.

'You English?'

'No, no, no.'

'American?'

'No, no.'

'Deutschland?'

'No.' We turned over and lay on our fronts. We were not the kind of girls to get picked up like that.

'Where you from? Tell us, where you from?'

'Irlanda,' Kathy answered at last. It seemed rather rude to totally ignore them. Besides they were very handsome, with their dark eyes and smooth tans.

'We students from Madrid,' the taller of the two said. 'We work here for the summer. He Pedro, me Jesus.' They smiled dazzlingly at us and offered their hands.

It seemed churlish not to take their hands and introduce ourselves.

When we went for a swim, Jesus and Pedro came whooping into the sea after us. They splashed and dived under the water, caught our ankles, pretending to be sharks, making us scream and laugh and splash back. They threw a ball to us and raced us along the sand, then bought us beer and fresh bread rolls stuffed with sausage and cheese. They wanted us to go out with them that night and, after a quick consultation, we agreed.

Back in the safety of our *pension* bedroom we sat on the sagging beds with the rickety iron bedsteads and agreed that they were very nice, gentlemanly, young men, and great fun. Besides, they were students, so it was perfectly respectable to go out with them. We both wished we had brought something more glamorous to wear, and spent ages trying on one another's clothes before we could decide what to put on. As we put the last touches to our hair, we made a pact that we would stick together during the evening, in case the boys tried anything on, later we could see, but tonight we'd stick together.

'You like to see Spanish dancing?' Jesus asked when he and Pedro arrived to pick us up.

'Oh yes, please,' I answered.

He took my arm politely and walked on the outside. Irishmen could do with a few lessons in manners from him, I thought. I was glad I got Jesus, because he was the one who had most English, and Kathy could speak to Pedro in Spanish.

They brought us to the oldest part of the town, away from the seafront, to a small bar with a tiny dais for the band, and a minute dancefloor. It was already filling up with Spaniards and a few tourists. I decided that this must be the real thing, and not just Spanish schmaltz put on for the tourists. We drank Cuba Libres and Kathy and Pedro chatted away in Spanish with a lot of laughter.

'You are from Irlanda?' Jesus said.

I smiled and nodded over the rim of my glass.

'Irlanda is Católica, like España, no?'

'Sí, yes it is.'

'You are Católica, too, no?'

'Sí. sí. Yes, I am.'

'Do you know La Virgen de la Montaña? he asked, and brought out his wallet. He drew out a picture of a statue of Our Lady, one of those highly ornate Spanish statues dressed in cloth-of-gold and jewels, with an oval face and large, liquid, glass eyes. 'She is the Madonna of my village,' he proclaimed, 'and I love her very much.' He kissed the picture and put it back in his wallet. 'In the time of the, how you call it, Pascua?'

'Easter,' I guessed, intelligently.

'Yes, in the time of Easter, we dress our little Madonna in very special clothes and bring her through all the village. Oh, she is so beautiful then.' He smiled and shook his head. 'You are very like her, very beautiful.'

I wasn't at all sure how I should take that, but at least I was grateful that as Jesus was obviously a devoted Catholic, I would have no trouble with him making passes at me later on. Then the dancers came: castanets ticka-ticked rapidly, heels drummed, hands clapped, skirts swirled, heads tossed, noses were looked down haughtily. I didn't want it ever to end.

'You can see we are a people of much passion, no?' Jesus said, when we were clapping till our hands were sore. 'You like the passion, no?' He was looking deep into my eyes.

'Oh yes,' I answered fervently, 'I think it's wonderful.'

'You are very beautiful, like my little Madonna.'

'Don't be silly.' I was embarrassed.

'You do not think so?' he asked, as though profoundly shocked that I should question it.

'Well, I mean, I'm all right, but I'm not beautiful.' I laughed at the idea, half-embarrassed, half-pleased.

'But your eyes, your eyes, they are so beautiful. You have the eyes of blue, like the sky, and the black hair with the white skin. In España this is not possible.'

'Oh, it's very ordinary in Ireland,' I said, thrilled to bits. I had never before received compliments like this from a man. Irishmen may have the gift of the gab, but they don't use it to flatter women. At least, none of the ones I know.

I didn't even consult Kathy before agreeing to meet Jesus again the next day when he had finished work in the hotel.

'Tomorrow we go dancing,' he said, as he left me to my door. He kissed my hand and looked longingly at me over my wrist bone. Then he plucked a flower from a bush that was trailing over a nearby wall. 'Keep this for me, blue eyes, black hair,' he said, as he gave it to me. 'Keep it close to your heart, and sleep with the small angels. I will dream of you all of the night.'

He was so serious I almost laughed. I wondered if Kathy could hear. Pedro was whispering urgently into her ear.

Back in our bare bedroom we rolled around laughing, thrilled with our success and pretending sophisticated detachment.

'You wouldn't want to believe a word they say,' said Kathy.

'Well, of course not. They're terrible flatterers, but a bit of a change from Irishmen.'

'God yes. I think all Irishmen should be deported for a minimum of five years so that they learn how to treat women,' said Kathy.

'Agreed, agreed. I know a few guys who would benefit from a few lessons from Jesus. A bit of flattery is really nice to get. Even if it's not true,' I added hastily.

We couldn't wait to meet them again.

The place we went to next night was the most romantic I'd ever seen. The dancefloor was hung round with coloured lanterns, and one side was open to the sea. We took a table on the balcony overlooking the beach. The Mediterranean lapped gently. Stars twinkled in a deep purple sky. A crescent moon hung over the water. The band, a collection of middle-aged men in cummerbunds and brylcreamed hair, played song after romantic song. What more could we ask for? As we danced Jesus drew me closer and closer. He sang the songs into my ear in a low throbbing voice, as though the words had been written especially for me and he had been waiting all his life to say them. I sighed with pleasure and moved a fraction closer. I could see Kathy dancing nearby, with her eyes closed and a blissful look on her face.

'Come with me to the sea and make a wish on the moon,' Jesus whispered.

What a romantic idea! I agreed immediately. We walked along in the starlight and Jesus told me again and in detail just how beautiful I was. He kissed my hand and worked his way up my arm to my lips. We kissed passionately for an eternity, and then his hands began to move down my body. I tried to stop him gently, but her persisted. I didn't want to stop him, but I was getting nervous that he was going too far. I had always thought of my body as being marked off in sections, like the illustrations of carcasses in a butcher's shop. My areas were clearly marked 'neutral', 'venial sin' and 'mortal sin'. I relented enough to let him touch the 'venial sin' bits, but when he determinedly began to enter the areas labelled 'mortal sin', I pulled away and stopped him firmly.

'Why you do this?' he asked, in a dismayed voice. 'What is wrong?'

'Nothing's wrong. I think I should go home now.'

'It is because you do not like me?' He sounded distraught.

'No, no. That's not true. Of course I like you,' I answered hastily.

'Why you stop me loving you?'

'Well, it's just that . . . oh, I don't know how to explain.'

'Is all right,' he said, moving away from me, 'no explain. I understand very well. You do not love me. You do not care for me. You are very cruel. Is all right. I understand. I love you, but you do not love me.'

'Oh, but Jesus, that's not true' I pleaded. I didn't want him to leave thinking that. 'But how can you say that you love me? After all, you do not know me very well. We only met yesterday.'

'It no matter how long. The heart do not have a clock. The heart know when it *loves*.' He held his hand dramatically to his heart. 'I love you, but you do not love me.'

'Of course I like you Jesus. You are a very attractive man, but . . .'

'But, but, but . . . but what?' he seemed to be getting angry.

'Well, I told you already. I am a Catholic.' I thought this should be explanation enough. After all, he was Catholic too. He must know the rules.

'You are Católica, sí, but you are very, very Católica, no?' he asked.

'How do you mean, very, very Catholic?'

'I mean, very Católica as the old women who pray and light candles to the Virgin.'

'Oh no. Not like that.' I rejected the idea of superstitious piety.

'Bueno, bueno,' he murmured, and began to kiss me again.

For the next ten days Kathy and I struggled nightly to preserve our virginity, and we succeeded. Jesus and Pedro were baffled at our attitude. They told us that English and German girls were only too willing to go to bed with them. 'In Ireland it is different,' we told them, with considerable pride.

Then it was time to start travelling north again. I refused to think of it as going home. It was just another phase of the holidays. I was determined not to allow any thought of home and work until we landed once again in Dun Laoghaire.

When we landed back in Ireland we came straight off the boat with just time for a quick wash before facing our classes for the next year. Oh boring, boring. Ireland seemed dull. No men passed remarks about us in the street. The weather was grey and damp.

A week later I met Gerry Murphy, whom I knew from college. He asked me out for a drink. We drove out to Howth in his father's car and parked near the harbour. He got out and I waited for him to come round and open my door for me. He crossed the street, and it was only when he had gone about twenty yards that he realised that I was not with him. He looked back and shouted:

'Come on. What's keeping you?'

I sighed, opened my own door and crossed over, leaving the car door open.

'Hey. What'd you do that for?' he asked, surprised.

'I got used to having doors opened and closed for me on the Continent,' I replied haughtily, 'where men *know* how to treat women.'

'Well, you're not on the Continent now,' he laughed, 'you'd better go and close the door.'

I did. Oh yes, I was back in Ireland all right.

*　　　*　　　*

3

ANOTHER NIGHT beside Oliver, lying as faraway from him as the bed would allow, I remembered Nora, Barbara and Norma, who led lives as different from mine as an Eskimo's, I realised that they had given me a point of real contact with the children I was now teaching. I get the same guilty thrill from my pupil' anarchic attitudes to life as I got the time Nora brought us off to buy sweets with money stolen from the Black Babies mission box.

I know that some of the things which the pupils of St Brigid's Special School have been up to are pretty hair-raising. After all that's often why they're there. And I know that unless you're very firm with them they'll walk all over you. But sometimes I can't help admiring their sheer ingenuity. One time some of the older girls decided to revenge themselves on the nuns for some injustice. Three of them stayed awake till after midnight when they were sure that everyone would be asleep. Then they got out of bed, sneaked through the door marked 'Convent', tiptoeing through that part of the house which is forbidden to all except the nuns. Noiselessly they went into each nun's bedroom and stole every set of false teeth in sight. The nuns slept soundly while the girls crept back into their part of the building and down to the furnace room where they destroyed all the dentures. Next day the nuns, gap-toothed and gummy, raged against the outrage. The lay staff kept their faces straight and clucked sympathetically. The girls all looked innocent. Sister Magdalen conducted a great inquisition but nobody split so she got angrier and angrier. Eventually somebody discovered an unlocked door in the basement and the crime was attributed to some unbalanced person who must have got in in the dead of the night. The girls looked more innocent than ever.

This was the kind of episode I would hear about whenever I took the class on an outing and had time to talk to them. It gave me a chance to get some idea of what made them do the crimes. 'Why do you steal handbags? Is it because you want the money?' I once asked. 'Ah yeah, miss, the money's all right,' I was told, 'but it's getting chased that's the best. It's great it is, running down Henry Street with an aul' wan chasin' after you, and she screechin' an' bawlin' an' wavin' her umbrella at you. An' you knowin' she'll never catch you.' Everyone nodded in agreement. 'An' then you can go down to the shops an' get chips an' burgers,' somebody added wistfully. Their crimes seemed funny and sad and curiously innocent when told from their point of view.

Oliver used to laugh whenever I told him these stories. Then he'd go all serious and complain about Irish hypocrisy, how this was supposed to be a Christian country and look what we did to the poor downtrodden. I used to think that meant he shared my views.

Before I met Oliver I sometimes took my class away for the weekend. We'd stay in a youth hostel and go walking or climbing. Since I'd met him I'd spent all the free time I could with Oliver. I thought that weekends were the time when couples did things together. Yet somehow these couple-type things for which I was making myself available never seemed to happen. Oliver always had paper-work to do and when it was finished all he ever wanted was to lounge in front of the television or read the inevitable newspapers. Well, I suppose it was the only time he had to relax, wasn't it?

He did cook Sunday lunch, an elaborate meal which involved sauces and salads and linen napkins. Although he often laughed that he'd left home to escape his mother's cooking, nevertheless he talked about the Sunday lunch back home in Sligo as though it was some sacred institution. I used to joke him that he had given up mass on Sundays in favour of lunch on Sundays. He didn't think that was funny. In the beginning I thought that Sunday morning in the kitchen sipping sherry together would be nice. I thought it would be a time for sharing feelings, for discussing ideas, a time to catch up on the things that had happened during the week. It didn't work out like that. Oliver didn't want idle chit-chat to distract him from his task. My job was to find the

Tobasco, weigh the flour, chop the vegetables, peel the grapes, not to sit round chattering and distracting the master chef. I often wondered what he'd do if I weren't there. Probably go out and buy a food processor.

'I'm thinking of taking my class away the weekend after next,' I told him in the morning over the toast and sugar-free pear and apple spread.

'You're what?'

'Taking my class youth hostelling for the weekend.'

'You're daft,' he pronounced, buttering another slice of toast.

'You could come if you liked,' I added hesitantly. 'It might be nice to get out in the air for a change.' I knew really that he wouldn't but I half hoped that he might.

He ignored my suggestion. 'What do you want to do that for?'

'Well I've always done it with other classes.'

'So?'

'Oliver, some of these kids have never been outside the city in their lives. It'll be an experience for them and will get them away from school for a while. Anyway I enjoy it too.'

'Oh I see, it's devotion to duty is it? Look Margaret, you do your stint with them during the week and I don't see why you should have to spend the weekend with them as well. You've nothing in common with them, I mean what on earth could a mature adult have in common with a lot of teenage delinquents?' He rose from the table and put on his jacket. 'And what about me?' he added peevishly. 'What am I supposed to do while you're away?'

'Oh Oliver, you know you always have things to do, work, television, the newspapers, I'm sure you'll be able to cope.'

'There's no need to be sarcastic, Margaret. You know perfectly well what I mean. What about the Sunday lunch? This means I'm going to have to eat it by myself!'

I kept quiet while he checked his briefcase and searched for his car keys otherwise I would have got a lot more sarcastic. I prided myself on not losing my temper and starting rows. But even as I smiled and kissed him goodbye, I sneered inwardly: poor Oliver he's going to have to eat his Sunday dinner all by himself. The tragedy of it! Oh, the heart bleeds! Really, sometimes he behaved like a spoiled child. I kicked one of his chairs in revenge.

Sister Magdalen didn't look at me when I went to ask her permission for the trip. 'Do you think it's wise, Miss McCabe?' She brushed a long elegant finger over her desk top and scrutinised it for invisible dust particles.

I must still be in her bad books, I thought, probably I was going to remain there forever. I had a sudden urge to run round to her side of the desk and peer up into her face to see if I could make her look at me, but I resisted it. 'Well it's worked out very well every other time,' I said instead.

'Hmmmm.'

She finished examining her finger and concentrated on a spot somewhere behind my left ear. I moved a little to be in her direct line of vision and her eye shifted again. Once, in the corridor, I had got her to do a complete turn about by shifting like this to catch her eye, but now the bookcase was in the way.

'I was just wondering about the wisdom of bringing Pat Walsh with you. She's an extremely difficult and troublesome child and could be a problem.'

'She'll probably be much more of a problem if she doesn't come, and besides, I usually find her reasonable enough if she's not bored.'

Sister Magdalen is no fool, she knew I was being indirectly critical of the school. I had once suggested to her that the girls could do with more stimulating activities out of school hours and was promptly told that it was none of my business. I could see the memory of that transgression in her eyes now, but there wasn't much she could do about it.

'Very well,' she said, sitting down and opening a roll book, 'if you're prepared to take that responsibility.'

On the way to the classroom I had a stab of panic about what I would do if Pat did decide to get obstreperous while we were away. I had once seen her lose her temper in the playground. She was like a demon: she screamed abuse and hit out all round her, attacking a much younger child. What if something like that happened in the youth hostel? Oh damn Sister Magdalen anyway, she could always undermine my confidence. Then I remembered that it was I who had calmed Pat that time. I felt a bit

brought me to meet any of them it would be some kind of sign that I really meant something to him. Now I saw that chance disappear again into the mists of the future.

On Friday, alone in bed I could think in comfort.

*   *   *

Every summer, after that first one with Jesus in Spain, I left the country and travelled. I became *blasé* about the naked Scandinavians and more expert in handling the amorous Latins. Every time I came back home I thought of taking off for a year and travelling round like so many of the people I'd met in the hostels, India maybe, or South America; but to do that, I'd have had to give up my job and mightn't have been able to get another one when I came back. Besides, what on earth would my parents have said, after they had put all that effort into making sure I got a good education. And anyway, how would I ever have got enough money together? I was doing OK, wasn't I? I didn't enjoy the teaching much, but it paid me enough to have a car and to travel in the summer. Those were my excuses.

At the time, I was still living at home with my parents. That's what everyone in Dublin did, stayed at home until they got married or emigrated. Kathy and I used to spend hours planning how we'd tell our parents that we were going into a flat. But when it came to the point neither of us ever had the courage: we were sure that they'd kick up a fuss about it, and besides, we'd probably get married sometime soon.

The problem about marrying was that I never met anybody that I wanted to marry. All the men I ever met were either boring or boorish, or both. That was until I met Colm, and my parents never liked him. I could never quite understand what their objection was, though my mother thought he had a sneaky expression and my father that he was too smart by half. I suspect they didn't think he was good enough for me because he didn't have a university degree. He did, however, have a low-slung sports car and lots of money, but I think they felt that money without education was suspect.

Colm ran a wine-importing business with his father. This meant that he travelled regularly to the Continent, and spoke fluent French. He was funny, intelligent and attractive. He called his car 'The Beast'. It had a front grill that looked like a row of shiny teeth ready to snap off the rear fender of any car which did not let him pass. It had one of those purry-growly engines which Colm liked to rev to a roar as he shot past wobbly Morris Minors and solid family saloons. At least once a week he took me out for a meal; being in the wine business, he fancied himself as something of a gourmet. He was constantly discovering little places where the food was wonderful, most were scattered in the hills to the south, or in the lush pastureland to the north of the city. Not one of them was nearer than thirty miles away, it meant that I got a mini Monte Carlo with every meal. The only problem about Colm was that he never made a pass at me – Kathy and I had agreed that while we didn't want men to pounce on us like maddened savages, we'd be very suspicious about a man who never made a pass at all – so there must be something wrong, I thought, and yet Colm seemed perfectly normal. Of course, he was very religious. Maybe that was it.

Most of the people with whom I was friendly considered themselves liberated Catholics, didn't get over-excited about missing mass on Sundays, thought the papal position on contraception was all wrong, and told funny stories about right-wing clerics. The rest claimed no religion at all. By now, I hovered between the two. *Humanae Vitae* had very definitely shaken my faith in the Church, but Colm was a Catholic in the old style. He always went to mass and regularly attended the Men's Sodality. Everyone I knew had given up sodalities years ago. In fact, I had thought they'd been abolished. I wondered if Colm was the 'good Catholic boy' whom Sister Evangeline used to tell us about, the kind we should look for and marry. She had illustrated her point by telling us the story of the young couple – the girl was a past pupil of St Saviour's – who had exchanged rosary beads on their wedding night. I had often told the story as an example of silly things nuns told you in school, but maybe I was wrong. Maybe Sister Evangeline was right, well . . . maybe. . . .

I had been going out with Colm for a few weeks when I decided that, no matter how good a Catholic he was, he could at least kiss me. Since the Vatican Council that could hardly be a sin. I wasn't going to try and tempt him into going too far, but surely a bit of kissing, and maybe a little hugging, would be nice. On the way home from the 'Stack of Barley', a little family restaurant which did incredible things with veal, I made the decision. I am going to stay in this car, I thought, until he kisses me, even if I have to stay all night; it was a beautiful May evening, and I thought it was about time his fancy turned to thoughts of love. When we got to my house he parked, as usual, outside the door. I noticed the flutter of drapery which told me that Mrs Duncan next door was still awake and checking what was going on. I settled down to wait. We enthused about the latest Beatles album. He told me funny stories about the customs men in France. I told him a funny story about the customs post in Irún. I changed my position several times to be sure to be within easy grab range. Colm went on to talk about the need for more ergonomically designed furniture and kitchen fittings. I agreed entirely with him. We got out more cigarettes and as he was lighting it for me I leaned closed and smiled enigmatically at him over the flame. Colm just leaned back against his door and talked on. This is getting ridiculous, I thought, it is men who are supposed to have all these rampant passions you hear about, women the ones who are supposed to be in control! I dropped my hand carelessly onto the seat beside him, to make it easy for him to take it as a first move. I could hardly make an obvious pass. I mean, I was doing everything I could, wasn't I?

The next time he lit a cigarette for me I threw maidenly modesty to the winds and held his hand while I smiled enigmatically over the flame. he stuck his cigarette hastily into the ashtray and kissed me, knocking the lighted cigarette into my lap. I jumped away to stop myself going up in flames. We stubbed the cigarettes and started again. He kept his lips firmly closed and pressed hard. I could feel the beginning of his stubble scrape my face. It was a bit like being pressed to a pebble-dash wall.

'We'd better not stay here,' he said hoarsely, glancing at my parents' bedroom curtains. He started up the car and drove down the road to a *cul-de-sac*, where he parked in shadow. Then he started pressing our faces together again. 'Oh, Margaret, Margaret,' he kept repeating, and held me tightly, so that my arms were pinnioned and I certainly could not lead him on. A garda on his beat flashed his torch in at us, and we were still there when he returned again.

The sky was lightening and I said I had to go. Colm made a final pebble-dash-wall assault on me and then drove me back. As I stood, easing my key quietly into the lock, I remember thinking that my face felt raw and my jaw felt like it might need special exercises. I stepped quietly into the hall.

'This is a lovely hour of the night to be coming home,' exclaimed my father's voice.

I looked up and there he was standing at the return of the stairs. I thought irrelevantly that he was standing the same way as he was in the army photograph taken when he was an officer during the Emergency. Only now he was wearing his crushed, red-and-white striped pyjamas. He was incandescent with rage.

'What kept you out till this hour of the night?' he demanded.

'I was just out with Colm, Daddy.'

'Hah! That fellow is it. And does he consider this a proper hour to bring any decent girl home?'

'We were just talking.'

'If you were just talking, why was it necessary to drive up to the house and then drive away again? Can you tell me that?'

'Well, we – '

'You needn't bother denying it. Your mother and I have been awake all night worrying about you. We heard that infernal car coming and going. You couldn't mistake it. Just what are that young man's intentions? Now answer me that!'

My mother had crept down the stairs behind him. She was in her nightdress, looking like a pale ghost in pink rollers. I could sense her worry. When Daddy got angry she got agitated and tried to placate everybody.

'He means are you and Colm going to get married,' she explained.

'I . . . I don't know. We haven't talked about that, I – '

'What do you mean, not talked about it? Haven't you just told me that you spent the past four hours talking. I know the kind of talking you two were up to, the kind of talk that leads to a hasty wedding, that's what it was.'

'Oh God, you've got it all wrong,' I said wearily.

'And don't you take the name of God in vain in this house,' he roared.

'Bernard, dear. Please take it easy. Remember what the doctor said about your blood pressure. Don't upset yourself,' Mammy soothed. 'It's just that he's worried about you. We were both worried,' she added to me.

'Please, I'm tired and I want to go to bed,' I said.

'And what about us?' Daddy raged on. 'How do you think we feel? Don't you think we're tired too? We've been worried sick about you, streeling in her at all hours, making a name for yourself in the neighbourhood.'

'Good night,' I said, and rushed for my bedroom.

'Good morning, more likely. Oh, I'll have a few words to say to that young man when I lay my hands on him! And you can tell him that from me,' he shouted through the closed door.

I could hear my mother making little cooing noises to try and calm him down. She was still at it when I fell asleep.

The next time I spoke to Colm on the phone I warned him not to come to the house. I would just die of embarrassment if Daddy started a scene. From then on, I got Colm to park in the parallel road while we said good night.

Somehow I had thought that Colm's kissing technique would improve with practice, but it didn't. Eventually, after a number of jaw-numbing sessions I decided to try a little education. I told him to relax and do nothing and I'd show him how I liked to be kissed. He groaned very satisfactorily.

Much later, he said, 'Now Margaret, I don't think we should go too far.'

I had no intention of going too far. I was fully prepared to wait until we got married.

A month later Colm told me that he didn't think we should continue to see one another. I was baffled. I couldn't work it out. We got on so well together. There had been no hint that anything was wrong.

'But why, Colm, why, what's the matter?' I begged.

'It's just that I don't think we're suited.'

'Not suited! Colm, I cannot believe that. We always get on so well together. We can make one another laugh. We always have fun together. What is it? I don't understand.'

'Well, it's just that you're so left-wing. I mean you're great fun and everything, but you're far too broadminded for me.'

I cried my eyes out for a month, and my parents, with monumental tact, never asked me a thing. Kathy consoled me by saying she thought he was far too conservative and narrow-minded for me, and anyway she had never really liked him that much. That was when I formally stopped being a Catholic. Colm was just the last straw.

Time passed and suddenly I was coming up to my thirtieth birthday. I was still at home with my parents. I was still in a boring job, and I was still a virgin. Kathy and I discussed it at length.

'But what would you really like to do?' she asked.

'Oh, I'd like to travel all over the world, write a book, paint pictures, take photographs, live with a man, have a ball,' I replied.

'Yeah, so would I,' she agreed.

Instead, we both changed our jobs.

I was turning the pages of the newspaper when I saw a notice about an education seminar. I thought it might be interesting, and I could probably get a few days off school to go to it.

It was at this seminar that I first met Sister Magdalen. She spoke to a packed audience on 'Children in Distress: the Education of the Emotionally Deprived'. Her speech was inspirational. She talked of her school and the children in it, children forgotten by society and sometimes even by their parents, children who, through neglect, turn to crime. She told us that these youngsters lack the experience of love in their lives, therefore, we could not expect them to behave normally towards a society which treats them so badly. She told us that her school was designed so that the children could, at last, get the experience of love. She talked about the joys and the difficulties. When she had finished she got a standing ovation, and many of the audience, including Kathy and I, had tears in our eyes.

'Wouldn't it be wonderful to work in that school,' I said, 'a change from the boring old daughters of the moneyed classes. It really could be a challenge.'

'I was thinking that very exact thing myself,' replied Kathy. 'If I get a chance, I think I'll ask her about jobs in her school.'

'But wouldn't you need special qualifications to get in there?'

'I don't know, Mag, but there can't be any harm I asking.'

Kathy was always better at sticking her neck out than me. During the lunch she went straight over to Sister Magdalen. 'Sister, I enjoyed your talk immensely,' she said, 'it really was quite inspirational.'

Sister Magdalen bowed her head modestly. 'I'm glad you enjoyed it.' She smiled.

'It really made me feel that I'd love to work with those children. Do you need any special qualifications for it?'

'The best qualification you could have is a good sense of humour and the ability to love,' she answered, smiling charmingly at both of us.

'If you're looking for staff, Sister, both Margaret and I would be interested.'

'Sister Magdalen laughed, a clear, delighted sound. 'It must be providence,' she said. 'As it happens, I will be looking for staff. We are extending the second level this year. Here,' she took out a notebook, 'let me have your names and addresses. I'll see that you are both interviewed. I can't do more than that. In the meantime, apply to the manager in the normal way.'

Hardly believing our luck, we thanked her profusely and told her once again how wonderful her lecture had been.

'There, I told you!' crowed Kathy. 'That was easy, wasn't it?'

'I'll tell you after the interviews,' I said, more cautiously, but in fact I was jealous that Kathy had taken the initiative and not me.

Sister Magdalen was as good as her word. We not only got the interviews, we got the jobs. For the first term in St Brigid's Special School I felt as though I was riding a bucking bronco. I got the first years, and taught them most subjects except gym, art and domestic science. I even had to teach them religious knowledge, that threw me somewhat, because I hadn't admitted to anyone except close friends that I wasn't a practising Catholic, it would have been as much as my job was worth. I got a book with all the information I needed in it, but I was left to struggle with my conscience. I decided eventually that the children's parents would want it, and when I read the religious knowledge book there wasn't anything in it that I couldn't at least half-agree with. I soon discovered that if you could survive the shock treatment the children handed out, deal justly and firmly with trouble, and be prepared to listen to each of them, there wasn't too much bother. I also discovered that you couldn't get away with sloppy teaching: they'd be bored in ten seconds and start making trouble. This meant that I had to be always thinking of new ways to present information. It was tiring, sometimes frustrating, but very exciting.

At the beginning of each term we had a staff meeting and occasionally, if Sister Magdalen had something special to tell us, she would call one during the term. The meetings usually consisted of her talking and the rest of us listening. Now and then a teacher was asked for her opinion on something, but there was never any real discussion.

One day, at the beginning of my first summer term, Geraldine Byrne came into the staffroom, balancing a pile of books as usual. She was the Union representative and talked about little else. She wore long baggy home-knit cardigans and was constantly pushing glasses back up her nose and lank hair out of her eyes. 'Staff meeting at three o'clock,' she said, trying to hold a cup of tea in one hand and hang on to the pile of books with the other.

'Staff meeting indeed!' sniffed Nora Harvey. 'Staff *lecture* is more like it.'

I didn't say anything. I thought that Nora had a point but I didn't like to criticise when I was only one of the newest members of the staff. It made me uneasy that Nora often seemed to be highly critical of Sister Magdalen. Not that she said all that much, just sat there in her beautifully tailored suits with her square sensible face and made the odd caustic comment. Usually I could see why she made the remarks, nevertheless I thought she was being over-critical.

'We should have meetings much more regularly, real meetings where we can discuss things properly,' said Geraldine.

'That's a good idea,' I said, 'it would be really interesting to have a chance to pool ideas for teaching, talk about school outings and things. You know, there's loads of things I'd like to hear all your opinions on.'

This staff meeting was like all the others: Sister Magdalen told us that she would like us to make sure that the children did not drop sweet papers in the corridors, to be sure that our classrooms were properly locked before we left, and so on. Finally she raised her head and smiled sweetly round the group to show that she had finished.

Nora Harvey spoke up. 'Sister, do you think it would be possible to have more frequent staff meetings? Perhaps a couple of times a term? They would be useful to discuss mutual problems and the staff could be informed of any events which are coming up.'

It sounded perfectly reasonable to me, but Sister Magdalen pursed her lips and sat in silence, looking at the floor. People shifted in their seats and looked uncomfortable. One of the major grumbles was that we were never told about visitors to the school; inspectors, students and overseas visitors were led into our classrooms without any notice. The silence stretched for so long that I just had to say something.

'I'm only a new staff member,' I started humbly, 'but I'd certainly welcome the chance to discuss problems. You know, things we all find difficult with these children. Maybe we could come up with some new ideas, some guidelines, that we could all use.' I shrugged and smiled ingratiatingly.

Nora grinned and gave me a thumbs-up sign, concealed from Sister Magdalen's view by her handbag.

The nun turned her gaze on me for a full minute. She looked hurt and surprised. 'If you're having any difficulties, Miss McCabe, you can always come to me. I am always ready to help any of my teachers. But you must remember that a teacher's job is to teach. It's my job to look after the guidelines.' She stopped and looked round the room. 'Is there anything else, ladies?'

There was nothing.

'Now you see what I mean,' said Nora to me on the way out. 'The woman is impossible. She will not discuss anything, and refuses to treat her teachers like intelligent human beings.'

I thought about it on the way home. In all logic Nora was right, but somehow when Sister Magdalen looked at me like that, all hurt, I felt just the way I did when Sister Dominic in school used to call me into her office. Somehow, I must have done wrong.

Three days later Sister Magdalen came into my classroom. 'I just called in to see how you are getting on,' she said, looking concerned. 'Are you having any difficulties in particular that you want to discuss?'

'Not really, Sister,' I replied, impressed by her concern for me. 'At the staff meeting I was just thinking of things in general. You know, like working out an agreed policy on how to deal with temper tantrums or outbursts of violence. Things like that.'

'Well, Margaret, if you have any serious problems of discipline, you can always send the child to me.'

That wasn't the point, but I decided not to argue with her. I was beginning to feel in the wrong again.

'Yes, Sister,' I said.

'I just noticed Miss Harvey this morning,' she added, 'I don't think she looks at all well. Maybe she's suffering from strain.' She smiled sweetly and left.

I was left with the impression that Nora might have a history of nervous trouble. Sister Magdalen should know, after all she was the expert on disturbed children, it was only natural that she would know about adults too.

'Has she told you yet that I might be suffering from 'strain?' Nora asked me at lunch time.

I wondered how on earth she could know. I must have looked stunned.

'I can see by your face that she has,' Nora laughed bitterly. 'Don't worry, I wasn't eavesdropping. That's what she usually tells new people about the troublemakers.'

'That's right,' nodded Geraldine eagerly, 'that means anyone who ever asks a simple question. This place is a dictatorship you know.'

'You're new and enthusiastic,' Nora continued, 'you think The Mag knows everything there is to be known about these kids, and that's the way she intends to keep it. So she undermines everybody who disagrees with her. Not directly, mind you, but by implication. If she can make you think that I'm off my rocker, then you won't listen to me, will you?'

'That's the way she works,' Geraldine hunched herself across the table in agreement, 'I've seen it happen before, and no doubt it will happen again. She doesn't seem to realise that everyone finds out about it in the end.'

'Geraldine, you know as well as I do that she does it because it works,' Nora said with a shrug, 'nobody ever disagrees publicly with her. We never get a chance to share ideas, so she's always the one with the wonderful suggestions. Sister Magdalen always knows what is best, just like God.'

I said nothing. I thought that maybe they were exaggerating. Sister Magdalen was a bit of an autocrat all right, but then it *was* she who had made the school the place it was, and she was its Principal.

After three years in St Brigid's I found that I got on very well with the girls, and often children came to tell me their troubles. I felt particularly pleased about that. It must mean that they trusted and liked me.

I had realised by then that the school wasn't nearly as ideal as it had sounded when I had first heard Sister Magdalen talk about it. Out of class, the girls were looked after by some elderly nuns who had been there in the time of the high walls and penitential attitudes. No amount of bright colours, potted plants or removing of walls could change their belief that the girls were, at best, unreliable and, at worst, downright evil. But they kept trying to make ladies out of them.

'But you can't make a silk purse out of a sow's ear,' Sister Scholastica used to sigh to me. She used to be a novice mistress in the days when novices were expected to give unquestioning obedience, whoever sent her to work in St Brigid's must have been revenging herself for an injustice in the novitiate. These girls were far from novice material, and poor old Scholastica could never adjust to that; she was tetchy and pernickety so the girls hated her, they did everything they could to make her life miserable, and she spent all her time punishing them. I suspect that she hated them as much as they hated her. It wasn't her fault really, she should never have been left there. Unfortunately, she was House Mistress for the girls in my class. 'The children in your class are appalling, absolutely appalling,' she used to say, every time she met me in the corridor, as though it were all my fault. 'Ah, they're not too bad when you get to know them,' I'd reply every time, trying not to feel guilty. 'Oh, I know them well enough. All I can say is that you must be very tolerant.' She didn't make it sound like a virtue. Where, I wondered, was all the love and understanding Sister Magdalen went on and on about? What about the support and the acceptance of the children as human beings in profound distress? As far as I could see, it stopped as soon as they left the classroom. A few times, things got so bad that I thought of complaining to Sister Magdalen, but I didn't like to complain about another member of staff. Besides, I reminded myself, nuns always stand up for nuns.

Then it all came to a head. Roisín Molloy was one of the most difficult and contrary children who ever came into the school. She was constantly in trouble, and because of her reputation, she was generally the first to be blamed when anything went wrong. She and Sister Scholastica were permanently at loggerheads. One day the nun accused her of stealing money from her office. Roisín blew up. Not that she wasn't capable of stealing – wasn't that the reason she was here in the first place – but this time she had been blamed in the wrong.

'She's a scheming bitch. She's a whore's melt. I hate her. I hate her,' she screamed at me.

When I got her calmed down, I heard the whole story. Not only had Roisín not been near the office, but everyone knew who had taken the money. I promised to talk to Sister Scholastica about it.

The nun needed delicate handling, so I explained the story as tactfully as possible, making sure that I didn't appear to blame her in any way.

'You're far too gullible,' she sniffed, when I'd finished. 'You should know by now that you can't believe a word they say, especially not that Roisín Molloy one. I think you'll find she's behind it all right.' She walked away.

At lunchtime she made Roisín eat her meal standing at the windowsill, and the girl came back to class like a walking devil.

'Maybe you should say something to Sister Magdalen,' I suggested, feeling sure that she could deal fairly with the situation. 'She's probably in her office now. Why don't you go down there.'

On my way home, Sister Magdalen called me. I had often heard Nora and Geraldine talk about her 'veiled look', but I'd never experienced it myself until now. Her face looked as though she had drawn a grey veil over it, and her eyes were fixed on a point on the wall just beyond my left ear.

'A child from your class came to me this afternoon,' she said in a dangerous voice. 'She told me that you had encouraged her to complain to me about her house mother. Is this correct?'

'Well, yes, but . . .' I began, rather taken aback.

'Sister Scholastica tells me that you undermine her authority.'

'Yes, I mean no, Sister, I mean I just wanted – '

'That's quite enough, Miss McCabe. I am shocked and saddened by your behaviour. I'm afraid your attitude has changed terribly since you came here. When you first came I thought I was lucky to get an enthusiastic, experienced teacher, but something has happened to change you. I am disappointed, very disappointed. Perhaps you are having difficulties in your life. Are you having boyfriend trouble?'

'No, no, Sister,' I dismissed the suggestion impatiently, 'but Roisín had a legitimate complaint. I think she deserves a hearing.'

'That, Miss McCabe, is my business, not yours.'

'But there's often trouble between the children and Sister . . . well, some of the out-of-school staff.'

'That is no business of the teachers, and I would remind you once again that your responsibility is to teach, not to run the school.'

'But Sister, it does affect what happens in class.'

'Miss McCabe, Margaret, I feel very saddened by your attitude. I don't know what has happened to make you so anti-clerical. Please remember that anything that happens outside your classroom is for me to deal with. All you need concern yourself with is teaching your class. That is all I have to say.' She turned and left.

I stood there for a minute, dumbfounded. Then I made my out to the teachers' cloakroom, still feeling numb. I couldn't believe that she would talk to me like that, without having listened to what I had to say.

'I've just had the length and breadth of The Mag's tongue,' I told Kathy and Nora, who were there combing their hair.

Nora frowned warningly at me, put her finger to her lips, and jerked her thumb at the toilet door. I got my coat on and when we were outside, Nora murmured, 'You can't be too careful. The walls have ears. Let's go for a drink and you can tell all.'

Mahony's pub was almost deserted at that hour of the afternoon. Nora looked under the seat and checked a nearby lamp as though looking for a bugging device.

'I wouldn't put it past her to have us all bugged,' she joked grimly, 'but seriously, Margaret, you'd want to be careful what you say in that school. There are always people who will tell it back to her.'

'Are you serious?' I asked, astonished.

'Oh yes. Some people want to keep in her good books, so they'd report it back if you picked your nose! Just be careful. That's all I'm telling you.'

I told them what had happened. By now the numbness had worn off and I was feeling both angry and helpless. 'She didn't even listen to what I had to say. She just attacked me and dismissed me like a bold schoolgirl. She even had the nerve to ask me if I was having boyfriend difficulties.'

'Isn't that what I told you. That's her style all right.'

'And the worst of it is, that I just stood there like a frightened rabbit and took it.'

'Oh, don't worry Margaret. There's nothing you can really do about it,' Nora consoled me. 'She has that affect on everyone. Don't try taking her on. She'll make your life hell. Sure no wonder you're in trouble. Doesn't she know that you're friends with me! I'm considered a troublemaker and a disturber of the lovely spirit of the school. Did you know that?'

'Why, what did you do wrong?' asked Kathy, all agog.

'Oh, I argued about the placement of some of the children. I disagreed about keeping a child back a year. You know, capital offences like that' Nora grinned.

'What about the Union?' Kathy persisted. 'Couldn't we get them to do something about it?'

'I'm not sure that it would do any of us any good,' Nora answered, 'she'd just say that we were interfering in matters which were outside our competence and domain.'

'And even if you did succeed with the Union,' I added gloomily, 'she'd only have her knife in you, and things would be worse.'

'I bet anything she won't speak directly to you for at least a month. All you'll get is the veiled look.'

'Come on, let's have another drink,' said Kathy.

'I hear you got the works yesterday,' Geraldine muttered on the way to class the next day. 'I hope at least you're in the Union.'

'Yes, I am,' I answered. 'I want to lodge a complaint that the Principal of the school is refusing to look at me.'

'Oh, so you're getting the full treatment.' She laughed.

'Yes, and I've decided to talk brightly to her every time I see her.'

'Good on you Margaret!' said Geraldine, and raised her thumb as she disappeared into her classroom.

Nora was right. For the next month Sister Magdalen suddenly found fascinating spots on the wall whenever I came into view. When I went to her with some minor query, she looked at a point beyond my left ear and answered as briefly as possible.

She had only begun to look at me again when I committed another offence. She came into my class to let me know the time the children were to go to confession and while she was there the angelus rang.

'Perhaps you would like to lead the angelus?' She smiled at me, her head to one side, her blue eyes beaming.

Oh my God, I thought, I hope I can remember the words. I never said the angelus with my class, because I knew the children would just horse around during it. Besides, I felt it would be hypocritical of me. It was enough to have to deal with religious knowledge. Sister Magdalen stood there, her eyes lowered and her hands joined, waiting for me to begin.

'The Angel of the Lord declared unto Mary,' I began.

'And she conceived of the Holy Ghost,' they all responded.

'Hail Mary, full of grace . . .'

All through the 'Hail Mary' I was frantically trying to remember the next bit. For the life of me I could not. I could feel a blush start at the base of my neck and work its way up to my face, one or two of the girls tittered nervously. Sister Magdalen's eyes opened wide in surprise and, after what seemed an eternity of silence, she took over and finished the prayer for me.

'Gosh, Sister, I went completely blank there for a moment,' I burbled guiltily as soon as it was over, 'it's most embarrassing. It happens to me sometimes like that when I go to introduce friends I've known for years and I suddenly cannot remember their names.' I smiled, and could feel the sweat breaking out.

'Introductions are not quite as important as prayers,' she replied with pursed lips, looking into the distance.

Next day she started walking up and down the corridor outside my classroom during the religious knowledge period. I could see her through the glass in the door. She stared balefully at me each time she passed. I was sure that she was trying to listen to what I was teaching but, even if she wasn't, it unnerved me to see Sister Magdalen's baleful blue eye slide by. I bought a colourful poster and stuck it on the inside of the glass. It didn't quite cover the whole pane. Sometimes I was sure I could see the glitter of her eye at the slit, and wondered if I were getting paranoid. Next time I saw the glitter, I opened the door suddenly. I wasn't paranoid. Sister Magdalen was out there, eavesdropping. She hurried away, fumbling in her pocket as though that were the real reason for her pause outside my door. At the next staff meeting, she reminded us that no amount of coloured posters could replace good, committed teaching. She looked directly at me as she said it.

At home I let my parents believe that I was still a good Catholic, although I think my mother suspected. She had given up reminding me of the May devotions and the nine First Fridays, and concentrated on making sure I remembered the Sundays and Holy Days of Obligation. 'What date is it?' she would say, *apropos* of nothing. 'Isn't tomorrow the feast of Corpus Christi? I almost forgot, Bernard, we'll have to get mass tomorrow.' She hadn't forgotten at all, and certainly my father needed no reminding. It was just Mammy, being subtle.

I had the *Diocesan Handbook*, which gave the times of masses in every church in the diocese. After a Sunday away from home, I would slip some reference into the conversation about the half-four in Ballinteer, or the six-thirty in Adam and Eve's. I could be subtle too. On the Sundays I spent at home I used to go out for a half an hour, to give the impression of being to mass. Usually I went for a walk, bought the Sunday papers and, when I got back home, avoided any embarrassing discussion about the sermon.

The Sunday after the angelus incident, the weather was wet and cold and I stayed at home all day. About seven o'clock in the evening, Mammy started being subtle.

'Imagine, ten past seven already!' she exclaimed in mock surprise. 'I can't remember what time the last mass is at. Is it half-seven or eight o'clock?'

As she and Daddy had been to mass that morning, it could only have been meant for me. My father preferred the Victorian patriarch approach.

'You haven't been to mass today, have you, Margaret?' He glanced at the kitchen clock. 'You'd better get the skates under you, or you'll be late.'

I felt like hitting him, like screaming at both of them. They're treating me like a child, I thought, and ground my teeth. I said nothing, got my coat and went out. It was dark and cold and pouring rain. A car passed and splashed me. I felt miserable. It wasn't a suitable night for walking. I decided that I might as well go to the church and keep dry.

It was three-quarters full and smelled of damp overcoats. People had left umbrellas to drip in the porch, and the back benches were crowded with the late-comers, yawning, slouching, looking around and waiting for the moment when their Sunday obligation would be done and they could hurry home to the fire and the telly. Men with nicotined fingers held their check caps in their hands and leaned against the back wall. Teenagers who wanted to look manly stood, feet well apart, hands on wrists and heads thrown back. I slipped into one of the back seats and looked around. Across the aisle I caught Mairín Weldon's eye; I had seen very little of her since we had left school, we had found new friends and only met occasionally. We still called to one another's houses from time to time, talked, and promised one another that it wouldn't be so long the next time. Although I knew a fair bit about her job and her boyfriends, I knew very little about how she now thought or felt.

Father Burke climbed asthmatically into the pulpit and stood there, recovering his breath. He was a large untidy man with a round pale face and dark wiry hair which stood up all round his bald crown. His wheezing was amplified through the microphone, building up an atmospere of impending doom. At last he spoke. ' "The wisdom of this world is foolishness with God", St Paul to the Corinthians,' he wheezed menacingly, paused and glowered round the church. The congregation coughed, blew their noses, shuffled their feet and shifted in their seats. They weren't particularly perturbed by his drama. It happened every week and they just wanted it over to get home. I settled down to be bored. 'There are some people,' he continued, 'who do not realise the foolishness of this world; some people who do not listen to their Church and its ministers; some people who think they know better than their priests, better than their bishops, and even better than the Pope himself. They consider themselves intellectuals, no less.' He was getting red in the face by now, working himself up. 'There are some people, in this very parish, maybe even in this very church at the moment, who are saying that Martin Luther may have had a point. Even saying that he might have been right.' He placed his hands on the pulpit and leaned forward to the microphone, his elbows sticking out at each side. 'Martin Luther', he roared at us, 'was a heretic, still is a heretic, and always will be a heretic.' he began banging the pulpit with his fist. 'He was wrong – ' He broke down, coughing and wheezing, ' – absolutely wrong.' He groped under his surplice for a handkerchief and gave way to an asthmatic spasm for a few minutes. I caught Mairín's eye and we both went into a fit of giggles. Imagine, Martin Luther in this day and age.

Mass eventually ended and I shuffled out with Mairín.

'What did you think of yer man?' I asked.

'Christ, it's no wonder the country's in the state it's in with the clergy preaching that kind of rubbish. And they talk about Ian Paisley!' I laughed.

'Margaret, it isn't funny, not really,' she wrinkled her nose wryly. 'I'm only here because of my father. He's always on at me about going to mass. We have endless rows about it. I refuse to go and he lectures me, so eventually I give in, just to shut him up. It's ridiculous that a grown woman cannot make up her own mind without her father interfering. I'm always furious with myself when it happens.'

'Gosh, I thought I was the only one that happened to,' I said. 'Usually I go out for a walk, but tonight it was just too wet.'

'Isn't it crazy though,' said Mairín, 'two mature adults acting like children. And we're not the only ones you know. There's the Halligan twins and Johnny Curran and Frieda Walsh. They're just the same, going to mass so that their mothers will feel that they have reared them properly. It's all bound up with the oppression of women you know.'

'Oh, come on, Mairín,' I protested.

'No, seriously Margaret, it is. It's only since I joined Women Together that I've begun to realise just how oppressed women are by a patriarchal society and, my God, but the Church is patriarchal.'

I sort of switched off at that point. I was all for women's liberation, but the jargon got me down.

'You know, if we lived in the country,' I said when she had finished, 'it would be much easier to leave home. In the country everyone expects you to leave home to study or to get a job, but when you live in Dublin you're expected to stay at home forever.'

'What you need, Margaret, is the support of other women,' she said earnestly. 'I'm much better able to confront my father since I joined Women Together. In fact, I'm thinking of leaving home soon.'

If it's such a great help, I thought sourly, what has you here in the church porch on a wet Sunday night? Well, maybe there was something in it, but I didn't think it could be all that easy. . . .

*   *   *

How nice to drift into dreams without the cacophony of Oliver's snores, that was my last thought as I spread myself luxuriously across the bed.

4

IT WAS A RELIEF too the next morning to be able to get ready without Oliver wondering where I'd put his shirt and what I'd done with his briefcase.

My girls were standing outside the main entrance of the school, craning their necks anxiously, impatient for me to arrive. They were surrounded by a rockery of bags: duffle bags, handbags, shopping bags and endless plastic bags bulging with naked sausages, packets of crisps and bottles of lemonade. They cheered when I got out of the car, and cheered again a few minutes later when Kathy drove up – Kathy and I had done a number of these trips together, I went when she took her class and she with me – and I was glad to have her bubbly company again. She was great with the kids and they loved her: she always got a kick out of egging them on to tell about some of the more outrageous escapades.

The girls were giddy as we loaded up the school bus. Andrea had to rush back to get her coat, Pat demanded a check of the plastic bags to be sure that no food had been left behind and Pearl, Angela and Natasha dcecided at the very last moment that they had to go to the toilet. That sparked off a general rush to the loos. Finally we were ready to go. The skies were grey and looked like rain but nobody cared. 'Please miss, will there be mad bulls in the country?' somebody asked as I was trying to negotiate through tricky city traffic. 'Oh miss, miss, my brother got chased by a mad bull in Finglas one time,' added somebody else. 'Miss, miss,' Pearl shook my shoulder, 'isn't it true that the country's riddled with ghosts? Isn't it, miss?' Through the rearview mirror I could see her eyes black and wide. 'Me mammy says that's why the culchies all come to Dublin! she added. 'Oh miss, will there be ghosts where we're going?' another asked. 'Oh miss, I don't want to go if there's ghosts.' They were enjoying scaring themselves. Kathy took charge of the situation by suggesting a song. So they sang and waved at buses, screamed insults at gardaí and made faces at ordinary passers-by. It was not the kind of behaviour that Sister Magdalen would have approved of but what she didn't know wouldn't hurt her. Even little Mary Haverty seemed to be enjoying herself. She was hardly rocking at all and once or twice I thought I heard her hum along with the singing.

Glendalough was at its most looming when we arrived. The mountains rose, steep and sombre on either side and the pewter lakes reflected the green-black pines.

'God!' exclaimed Angela, climbing out of the bus and looking around her, 'The country's awful big!' She wrapped her arms round her as though for protection.

In the distance the round tower and monastic remains may have been dreaming of saintly hermits and the hum of learning, of treasured chalices and of Viking raids, but the pupils of St Brigid's were thinking only of fun. For the rest of the day we played hide-and-seek in the graveyard, walked by the lakes, chased through the trees and jumped from rock to rock in mountainy streams. 'Well, one thing you can be sure of,' Kathy said to me, 'there's no fear of them getting lost, they're too afraid to stray far.' It was true, they seemed nervous without streets and buildings to mark their territory and convinced that nature, unruly and untamed, would grab them and gobble them up like the witch in Hansel and Gretel.

Back in the youth hostel that evening, Pat took Kathy and me by the wrist and sat us down at a table. 'Youse are to sit here, miss,' she said, 'we'll cook for you.'

'That's right, miss, we have it all worked out,' agreed Natasha, and the others nodded enthusiastically.

'Fate worse than death,' murmured Kathy into my ear, 'but we'll just have to be brave.'

Pat clipped back her fair hair behind her ears, rolled up her sleeves and started organising. With a lot of shouting and pucking she arranged the girls, two to a gas ring, and distributed eggs, sausages, beans and potatoes to be cooked. She directed the boiling of kettles and kept a sisterly eye on Mary Haverty, who was supposed to be minding a pan of sausages but kept rocking from foot to foot, looking lost and letting the sausages burn.

'I wish Sister Magdalen were here to see them now,' I said to Kathy.

'No you do not, you clown,' she replied, 'you wish she could see what they are capable of but you wouldn't really want her here.'

'Right,' I agreed.

Later we sat round the table littered with the debris of the meal.

Pearl speared the last of the half-burnt sausages from the congealing grease. 'That was the very best dinner I ever had,' she sighed dreamily.

'Even better than the chipper,' said Angela.

'OK, ladies,' Kathy addressed the group, 'how about a walk in the dark? Anybody on for that?'

'Oh yeah, that'd be great, miss,' they chorused, jumping up enthusiastically, their eyes wide with anticipation.

'But I think we'd better get the washing-up done first.'

They moaned but nevertheless started to collect the dishes.

A wind had risen and the moon shone through racing clouds. The girls were both thrilled at their courage for going out in the country in the dark without street lights, and rather afraid of what might happen to them. They huddled together in groups, linking arms for comfort; each time the wind sighed and whispered they clutched one another more tightly. When an unseen cow mooed from behind a hedge they jumped and screamed and ran down the road; they saw ghosts in every shadow and heard the moaning of lost souls in every sound. They were glad enough to get back to the hostel and play cards and sing till it was time to go to bed.

After Sunday mass we were to climb a mountain. It was to be the highlight of the trip. We reached the edge of a pine plantation and it was time to start climbing. I directed them to climb along the edge of the forest.

'Up there?' squeaked Andrea, pointing up the slope.

'Is there no road, miss?' asked Pat.

'No Pat, there's no road.'

'No road!' Her eyes opened wide in disbelief. 'You mean we're going to have to climb through all that muck with no path or nothin'?'

'Exactly. That's why I told you that your pink, high-heeled ankle boots wouldn't do.'

'Jaysus, it's no wonder culchies are thick.'

'And it's no wonder they think Dublin jackeens like you are right eejits. Looking for a road up a mountain! Next thing you'll want Space Invaders and a Burgerland. Come on, up you go.'

We climbed up past the trees and on to the copper brown mountain. They weren't used to this kind of exercise, the bracken tore at their legs and their feet got wet in the boggy parts, but they kept going. They were determined to get to the top. As I climbed the last lung-pumping slope a couple of heads appeared over the edge and screamed, 'We beat you, miss, we beat you, we're the winners.' I plodded on, shepherding the stragglers who couldn't keep up with the main group. From the top you could see mountains in every direction: brown, burnt orange, black and grey sweeping away into the clouds. The wind was sharp and penetrating as we huddled together in the lee of an outcrop of granite, eating our squashed sandwiches. The girls drank fizzy lemonade but Kathy had brought a thermos of coffee for the two of us. 'Here, drink that up,' she said, handing me a mug, 'it would give you terminal hypothermia just looking at them lowering that stuff.' Not wanting to miss out on the educational opportunity, I enthused about the view and demonstrated the use of a compass. Nobody was interested, they were much more concerned that there wasn't a nearby toilet. They were appalled when I told them that they'd just have to go there on the side of the mountain. When eventually they got used to the idea, they set up an elaborate look-out system to make sure they wouldn't be overseen. They didn't seem to realise that there was nobody around but themselves.

On the way back down the rain caught us. It slashed across the wide mountain, jabbing at our eyes and making it difficult to see where we were going. By the time we got back to the path we were soaked through. When we reached a stream we didn't even bother to use the stepping stones but just waded miserably through. Pat slipped and fell, splashing down on her backside.

Here comes trouble, I thought, but she just sat there laughing.

'It doesn't matter,' she called, not attempting to get up. 'I was so wet anyway, it doesn't matter a fuck.'

She started scooping up handfulls of water and throwing them at her friends. Next thing they were all in there flailing around, slithering and slipping and having a glorious water fight.

'Oh I do wish Sister Magdalen were here to see them now,' Kathy said to me in mock-serious tones.

'Christ, can you imagine! She'd have a fit. I hope they all remembered to bring a change of clothes.'

As a result of the rain we were back in the hostel much earlier than I had anticipated. Between all of us there were enough spare clothes to make everyone dry and decent. The hostel was filling up with other climbers down from the mountains, all wanting to change their clothes and make meals. There seemed nothing for it but to go back home.

'What'll we do now, miss,' Pearl asked when we had all finished cups of tea.

'I think we'll just have to go back to school, it's too wet to stay here.'

There was a chorus of protest.

'Aah, miss, that's not fair.'

'You promised, miss, that we wouldn't go back till late.'

'Why can't we go back to town and go to the Arcade to play Space Invaders?' I could see trouble on the way. I knew for sure that the last thing I should do was let them loose in Dublin. As sure as anything, somebody would decide to run away, so I'd have to tell the police and Sister Magdalen would need no further proof of my unreliability. Then I remembered that Oliver wouldn't be back till late. His flight wasn't due until ten-fifty and the girls had to be back to school by eight o'clock. Why not.

'How would you like to come back to my house?' I asked.

'Oh yes, miss, please, miss.'

They piled happily into the bus.

'Will your fella be there, miss?' asked Pat.

'What's your fella like, miss?' Natasha wanted to know.

'Is he good-lookin', miss?'

'No, my fella won't be there and you'll have to make do with whatever food you have left over because I haven't enough in the house to feed all you lot.'

'Where's Oliver?' Kathy asked me.

'He's gone to London to see his brother,' I answered casually. 'He said he'd be lonely weithout me.'

'Lucky you, my fella thought he'd never see the back of me so he could get out to play golf with his cronies.'

I wanted to tell her right there how it really was between me and Oliver, but somehow I couldn't. Part of me felt that it would be somehow disloyal and part of me thought that actually saying it out loud would be an admission of failure. I couldn't believe yet that I'd failed with Oliver; it was just that he needed a bit more time to appreciate me. I knew that some of his previous girlfriends had treated him very badly and he needed time to recover from those hurts, to realise that I wasn't like that and he could trust me. Well that's what I told myself anyway.

Back at the house, the girls were like bees on a posy, incapable of staying still for a moment. They pulled out books, examined knick-knacks, ran up and down the stairs, went to the toilet, peered into cupboards and tiptoed into the bedrooms. I got some of them to prepare food and make tea, and tried to keep the rest of them in the sitting-room. Kathy had gone on home so I was alone. 'Your house is gorgeous, miss, so it is,' they kept telling me. I looked around and understood why they might think that but it didn't reflect much of me. Actually I didn't like Oliver's taste in furnishings, all that old-gold velvet and imitation antiques.

I didn't hear him come in. The first I knew was when I heard him call out: 'What the hell! What's going on? Margaret, where are you?' He put his head round the living-room door. 'Jesus H. Christ,' he exclaimed, looking round the room, 'what's the big idea?'

'Oh Oliver!' I jumped up guiltily – it was his house after all – and drew him out into the hall to explain what had happened.

'Jesus, Margaret, I don't get it. I come back early specially to see you, and what happens? Kids crawling all over the furniture. What kind of welcome is that?'

'But Oliver, you said you wouldn't be back till late, how was I to know?'

'Look Margaret, just get them out of this house as fast as you can.'

'Well you'll have to wait till they've had a cup of tea and something to eat.'

'OK, OK, just make it as quick as possible, I don't want my house crawling with borstal brats.'

I didn't think it was the right time to argue with him on that one. I let him go into the living-room and sit down with the girls. He'll like them when he gets talking to them, I assured myself, and went to see how things were going on in the kitchen.

When the food was ready Oliver was holding court from his favourite armchair. The girls were round him in a semicircle and he treated them like ladies, handing them cups of tea and offering sandwiches. He seemed to be getting on really well with them, back-chatting and leg-pulling. He even seemed to be enjoying it, it was a long time since I'd seen him so relaxed and humorous.

'Hey, miss,' called Pearl as I was pouring out tea, 'your fella won't believe us.'

'What is it?' I asked, curious and amused.

'Miss, he won't give us his car number,' explained Pearl.

'We want the number to make sure his car won't get done,' Pat added. She turned to Oliver, explaining patiently as though to a retarded child: 'Look, you just give us the number of the car, we pass it around, tell them you're a friend, and you're safe.'

'Safe my eye!' said Oliver. 'Stolen more likely.'

'No, no they won't touch it 'cause I'll burst their faces if they do.' Pat raised a clenched fist, 'I'd fuckin' kick their heads in if they laid a finger on one of my friend's cars.'

'That's right, that's right, they're all afraid of her, even the boys,' Angela assured us, and I could see why.

'Ah go on out of that,' said Oliver, rising from his chair.

'Honest, mister, honest, me an' me brothers an' a whole gang of us do cars. Cross me heart and hope to die.' Pat licked her middle finger and crossed her throat. 'It's great, it is,' she continued, 'we do the cars and then go down the Naas. You know, the Naas Road. Wally drives, he's the biggest. Vroom vroom seventy, vroom, vroom vroom eighty. One time we done a ton in a big Volvo.'

Pat was getting carried away by her memories and Oliver was

looking shocked.

'But we wouldn't ever nick a car off a friend, I swear to God! May He strike me down if it's a word of a lie!' She cast her eyes to the ceiling and crossed her throat once again.

'I'll have to go upstairs and change,' said Oliver, and he beckoned me out of the room. 'Get them out of here as fast as you can,' was all he said, and went up the stairs two at a time.

It was about time for us to go anyway so I rounded up the girls, made sure that they left the place scrupulously tidy so that Oliver couldn't complain, and drove them back to the school.

Sister Magdalen was reading her Office when we arrived, pacing the main corridor ritualistically. 'Well girls, did you enjoy yourselves?' she asked.

'Oh yes, sister, it was great.'

'We climbed a mountain.'

'An' we cooked our own meals.'

'An' sister, we got soakin' wet so we did.'

'I think they should have their clothes properly dried. We got caught in very heavy rain, sister,' I added by way of explanation.

'I hope none of the children catch a chill,' was her only reply, and she turned away to tell the girls to take their clothes to the drying-room in the laundry.

That's all! No thank you, no recognition that I'd given up my whole weekend. Not that I was looking for gratitude, but it would be nice if she could at least be pleasant, and a little gratitude would be all right too.

Oliver wasn't much better. 'I came home early specially,' he ranted at me the minute I returned, 'and what do I find? The house crawling with juvenile delinquents and car thieves. How do I know they haven't ransacked the house?'

'Oliver, all you have to do is look around you. It is quite obvious that the house hasn't been ransacked.'

'OK, but how do I know that they haven't nicked some stuff?'

'They wouldn't do that here,' I said wearily, 'I'm a friend and they think you're a friend too and they wouldn't do it to a friend, besides they know they'd get into trouble over it.'

'Well, I wouldn't want to trust them too far. Didn't you hear them, self-confessed robbers. They'd whip the eye out of your head if you weren't looking. I'll get a new lock put on the front door in the morning, just in case.'

'Oliver, please, I'm tired. I've had a tough weekend.'

'Who's fault is that anyway? You could have come to London with me instead!'

I took a deep breath and held my patience. He turned on the television and we watched in silence. Later he showed me the new set of super-sharp, stainless-steel kitchen knives which he had bought in London. I hoped it wasn't significant. And he complained about the inefficient mix-up at the airport, which meant that he had to come back on an earlier flight than he had intended. So much for coming back specially to see me.

I lay beside him feeling miserable, waiting for him to drop off to sleep so that I could turn off the light. What am I doing here, I wondered. Nothing seemed to be happening the way I thought it would. Where had I gone wrong?

*   *   *

It was the April before I met Oliver and Kathy and I were wondering what on earth she'd wear to her cousin's wedding. She had come round to my house to see if there was anything she could borrow.

'I've no intention of spending pots of money on a new outfit. I need the money if I'm to get away this summer, and anyway I don't like her very much.'

'You never know, Kathy,' I warned, 'you might meet a nice man there.'

'No, there's no chance of that. It'll be all aunts and uncles and elderly friends of the family.'

'Still, perhaps some of the groom's relatives will be eligible bachelors.'

'Now, Mag, you should know at this stage that there aren't too many gallant knights on white chargers around, and they don't go to family weddings.'

'Well, keep your eye out for the horse, anyway.'

We both laughed and I opened up my wardrobe.

'I thought your blue skirt and top might be nice,' Kathy said, poking through my clothes.

It looked terrible on her.

'Here, try the red silk instead.'

'No, it wouldn't suit me.'

'Well, try it anyway.'

She looked stunning in it, but wasn't sure if she could carry it off. I talked her into it.

After the wedding she telephoned me. 'Margaret, you'll never guess!' she bubbled. 'You were right! I met this fabulous man at the wedding.'

'Terrific. Tell me all about it.'

'Well, his name is Tom. He's an engineer and, surprise, surprise, he's not married. He thought I looked great in your dress!'

'Are you seeing him again?'

'Yes, I'm seeing him again tonight. That's if he turns up. You never know with Irishmen.'

He did turn up, and from then on I seldom saw Kathy outside school. She spent as much time as possible with Tom. Each day at lunchtime she'd tell me how it was going. Soon they were thinking about getting engaged. I was pleased for her, and a bit resentful that my long-standing friend had deserted me. But in her place I would have done the same.

Because Kathy was no longer around, I began to see more of Mairín. I didn't feel all that comfortable with her. She made me feel frivolous because I didn't constantly want to discuss the oppression of women. I knew that women needed liberating and that Irish ones needed it more than many, but I often wished she wouldn't take it so deadly serious.

Listening to Mairín, I began to feel that I ought to join a women's group. I supposed guiltily that I should be doing something for liberation. I decided to go to my first meeting of Women Together more out of a sense of duty than anything else. Mairín was delighted.

'Great,' she said, when I told her. 'We badly need help. You know the Minister for Health is going to address a medical conference at Jury's in two weeks.'

Mairín always assumed that I knew things like that, but I never did, and it always made me feel like an unaware slob.

'Ah ha?' I said non-commitedly.

'He has done absolutely nothing since he took office about the ban on contraception, and the medical profession just sits back and doesn't try to put on any pressure for a change in the law. It's the ideal place to protest. It's not just us. All the women's groups will be joining in.'

'Really? That's marvellous,' I enthused. 'You mean all the women's organisations will be there protesting? Fantastic!' I hadn't realised I was that out of contact with public opinion.

'Well, not all women's groups. Most of them would be too afraid of what people would say about them, or of losing their jobs if they were seen marching in favour of contraception, but all the feminist groups will be there.'

That was rather different.

'We need help making posters and placards, and we need as many women as possible to turn up.'

Women Together met in a room over a shop in the city centre. The stairs leading up to it was bare and the paint was peeling off the walls. A fly-specked, yellowing bulb glinted through a torn paper lampshade dangling over the landing outside. The room itself was better. It had been painted white and there were lots of posters on the wall. The furniture was old but serviceable.

When I arrived five or six women were sitting around, chatting and smoking. Mairín wasn't there yet and I felt a bit awkward, not knowing anyone. I moved over to the group and smiled. A motherly woman with untidy hair and a cigarette dangling from her lip invited me to sit beside her. She told me her name was Fran. A tall, thin girl came in with a large roll of cardboard.

'That's Harriet,' said Fran pointing to her, 'and that's Mairín Weldon, our Chairperson,' she added, indicating my friend, who had come in carrying several pieces of wood.

'Yes, I know Mairín,' I said, 'she used to be a neighbour of mine before she moved to the flat.'

By the end of the evening I had learned more about contraception in Ireland than I'd ever known before. As we worked away painting slogans and making placards, the women chatted and told me some of the problems of trying to limit a family in a country which considers contraceptives either illegal or sinful, or both. I was mystified by one slogan which read: 'CLING FILM - AN IRISH SOLUTION TO AN IRISH PROBLEM'.

'What does that mean?' I asked the woman who was painting

it.

'Cling film is what the kids use now for condoms.'

'Gee, I never knew that. Does it work?'

She laughed and patted my arm, 'I wouldn't depend on it myself!'

'WORKING WOMBS WANT A REST', Fran was painting on her poster. She gave me a blow by blow account of her nine pregnancies and their hideous complications. She told me of her doctor's assurance that the best thing she could use was the rhythm method. 'By the time I was thirty-one,' she informed me, 'I had four children on ignorance, three on the rhythm and three on Billings. Then I had the sense to change my doctor. He arranged for me to go to England and to have my tubes tied. It was expensive, but worth every penny.'

I knew that there were family planning clinics, but I'd forgotten that, strictly speaking, they were illegal and could be closed without warning.

'And even then lots of people don't even know where they are,' Mairín reminded me, 'and if you live outside the cities then that's just tough. You have nothing.'

'But surely, if you really want to get contraceptives you can come up to Dublin for them?'

'Not if you're poor, live in the heart of the country, have no transport, and your husband disapproves,' Mairín replied grimly. 'But that's not the point. Contraceptives should be legally available. If you won't use them because of your own moral beliefs, that's fine. Nobody's going to force you. All we want is that everyone should have the choice.'

Of course I'd never been faced with the problem. My sister Lucy and I were never on intimate enough terms to discuss it, and Patrick and Helen had always made it clear that they didn't intend to have more than two children. I had just assumed that there wasn't really a problem. 'What about contraceptives for single people?' I asked.

'Of course single people must be included,' chipped in Fran, 'but I wouldn't be caught saying that in public. I'd be hanged, drawn and quartered by a posse of Catholic Mothers of Ten.'

'Margaret, be very careful what you say in public,' Mairín warned solemnly. 'Someone would be sure to accuse us of corrupting the young. Just stick to the need for a change in the law to give women a choice.'

It sounded as though she expected me to go out and campaign immediately. I had no intention of saying anything to anybody. It was only the other day that Sister Magdalen had said that she had heard that there were family planning clinics in Dublin and what on earth was the country coming to. I didn't think it would do me any good at all if she knew that I was involved in this protest.

I wasn't so sure about my parents' attitudes. During a TV debate on the subject, my father left the room without any comment, but when he'd gone my mother remarked grimly, 'Women need some sort of protection against . . . well . . . . It's impossible to stop a man when he gets *that* into his head. I don't think the Pope really knows what it's like.' Still, I didn't think she'd approve of me being actively involved.

On the day of the Minister's speech about fifty women turned up to demonstrate. Press photographers came along and snapped us. My placard said 'IF MEN GOT PREGNANT, THE LAW WOULD BE CHANGED'. I held it towards the cameras so that it would be seen, and made sure that it covered my face as well. I didn't want anybody to recognise me in the newspapers.

The Minister arrived in the black State car. We unrolled a banner, waved our placards and shouted slogans. He stepped out of the car, smiled and waved as though we were his fan club. He shook the hand of a nervous-looking grey-suited doctor who was waiting for him. They disappeared through the swing doors of the hotel, and that was that. I thought it was a bit of an anti-climax. Now we had to settle down for the long wait while the Minister ate dinner and made a speech. We walked up and down, talking and laughing. There were a couple of gardaí on duty, who watched benignly. Visitors to the hotel looked curiously at us. Some smiled encouragingly. Others ignored us. 'There they are!' a strident voice called. I looked up and saw a crowd approach us. They looked as though they had riot shields. For a moment I thought it must be the police come to arrest us. I had a panicky flash of *Evening Press* headlines: 'Teacher Arrested', and wondered briefly if I could be sacked for it.

As they came nearer I realised that they were not the police at all but a group of people, each carrying a shield-shaped placard saying: 'GUARDIANS OF THE IRISH FAMILY'. There was something odd about the group, and it took me a while to realise that a considerable number of them were only children.

The leader was a solid woman with a voluminous grey tweed coat flapping around her. Underneath the coat she wore an apron over her jumper and skirt. Her hair was drawn back in a severe, grey bun and her face was as red as a turkey-cocks. There were five or six other women, a couple of men – one of whom appeared to be the husband of the tweed-coated woman and was huge, red-faced and tweedy too – and the rest were children of all ages.

'They look like Tweedledum and Tweedledee, don't they?' said Fran to me. 'That's Mr and Mrs Bradley.'

'Do you know them?' I asked.

'Oh, yes, they're the Guardians. They turn up at everything organised in favour of family planning, and they always bring their children.'

'She-devils,' screamed Mrs Bradley. 'She-devils, she-devils, she-devils,' the rest of the group took up the chant and banged on their shields, which I now realised were made of solid plastic. At a signal from Mrs Bradley they stopped and she beckoned one of the boys forward. Mr Bradley produced a megaphone and gave it to the boy, who began to speak.

I couldn't believe my eyes and ears. The boy was no more than twelve or thirteen and here he was addressing adult women on family life and the detrimental effect which contraception has on it. It seemed obvious that he had learned the speech by heart. Occasionally he forgot his lines and had to turn to his parents, who leaned forward and gave him the next line.

Next, a girl of about eight was called on. By now an amused crowd had gathered and photographers were taking pictures from all angles. Finally, Mrs Bradley took up the megaphone and declaimed. She quoted from the gospels of St Paul, the Apocalypse and the encyclicals of every pope from St Peter on. People were beginning to lose interest and move away. We continued walking up and down with our placards. When she'd finished, she stepped back beside her husband and started another chant.

'Scarlet women!' she bellowed through the megaphone. 'Scarlet wo-men, scar-let wo-men,' chanted all her cronies and their children banging on their shields. Suddenly, from somewhere behind her own shield, she whipped out an aerosol can, rushed forward and began to spray us with red paint. We lowered our placards for protection, and scattered.

The gardai, who had been standing nearby, after a moment's paralysis, dashed over to stop her. She whipped around with her finger still on the spray button and hit them in the face with the paint. It looked as though they were dripping blood. She gasped when she saw what she'd done, dropped the can and clapped her hand over her mouth. The photographers were going wild with delight, clicking and flashing in all directions.

'Come along now,' said one of the gardaí, wiping the paint out of his eyes.

'I'm sorry, officer, I'm sorry, I didn't mean to get you. You see I was doing God's work. Those women are doing the work of the Devil.'

'I'm afraid I'm going to have to arrest you anyway,' said the garda.

She stepped back on to the paint can, slipped and fell backwards with her legs in the air, exposing her sensible, sky-blue, interlock knickers. The policemen, paint still smeared all over their faces, helped her up and marched her away, to the shrieks and protests of her husband, friends and children.

'ARRESTED WHILE DOING GOD'S WORK', said the headline over the photograph of Mrs Bradley spraying paint at the gardaí. 'STRUCK BY THE WRATH OF GOD', said another showing her, legs in the air, with acres of knicker on display. Women Together ordered copies of the photographs and pinned them over the mantlepiece in our meeting room.

'That was hilarious, when Mrs B. attacked the policeman,' I said at our next meeting.

Mairín, Fran and Harriet were not amused.

'Mrs Bradley grabbed all the headlines,' Harriet rebuked me, 'and the protest itself got very little serious coverage.'

I was kind of glad. It meant that my face didn't appear. For the moment, I preferred to do good by stealth.

I was wondering what I'd do for the summer holidays now that Kathy was involved with Tom. I knew they were planning to go on holidays together. Then Mairín announced at a meeting that we would be able to get extra rooms in the building if we were prepared to repair and redecorate them ourselves. I volunteered to help during my summer holidays.

Fran, Harriet and I were the only ones who were free during the day, so we did a lot of the work. Both of them seemed to know how to do everything from stripping wallpaper to carpentry and plumbing. I just did as I was told.

'Where did you two learn all this?' I asked as I broke yet another nail sandpapering the window frame.

'If you were married to my fella, you'd soon have to learn to do it too,' Fran said. 'He couldn't hammer a nail in if you paid him. He'd be afraid he'd injure his pint-lifting arm!'

'How about you, Harriet?'

'I went to the tech' and found out,' she replied shortly, and I felt like a silly, middle-class slob.

'You wouldn't want to be depending on men to get things done for you, or for anything else for that matter,' continued Fran, 'I've never met one you could rely on.'

Harriet nodded in grim agreement.

'Ah, no, Fran. I don't think that's completely fair,' I burst out. 'Aren't women often their own worst enemies?'

'Internalised oppression,' Harriet snapped.

There were times when I didn't think I was feminist enough for these women. I continued sanding the window frame, feeling very unliberated, very middle-class, very stereotyped. And yet somehow, I felt that there was truth in what I was saying. They seemed to think I was blaming women. I wasn't. It was just that I thought it wasn't good enough to do nothing except complain. Surely we should be doing something positive as well.

When the rooms were ready we had a party. Everyone could bring their friends, as long as they were women. I tried to get Kathy to come, but she said hen parties always reminded her of those awful evenings before someone gets married and we all sat around in our good clothes, admiring the presents and cooing over the wedding dress. 'I don't think it will be like that,' I assured her, but she didn't come. She had a date with Tom.

The instant I came in the door I knew I was wrongly dressed. I wore a silky turquoise dress with gold trimmings and dangly gold earrings. I looked around the room and saw only navy cords, dungarees and large grey pullovers. Well, there were a few people dressed up, but we were in the minority. I wondered guiltily if it was unfeminist to dress up, and helped myself to a glass of wine.

'Why, hello, I don't think I've seen you around before.' The voice was so deep that for a moment I thought it was a man. I looked around and saw a small stocky woman in fatigues and army boots. She stood with her feet planted well apart and a pint glass of Guinness in her hand. 'My name is Marjorie,' she said. 'Who are you?' 'I'm Margaret,' I smiled back, but something about her made me feel uneasy.

'How is it I've never met you before?'

'I don't know. I only joined a couple of months ago.' I had a distinct feeling that I was being chatted up, and I didn't quite know what to do about it. I mean, if it was a man it would be different. I'd know what to do. But a woman! I excused myself and went over to talk to Mairín.

'I see Marjorie has been chatting you up,' she laughed. 'Don't worry. She chats up everybody.'

'Is she, you know, lesbian?' I asked, watching her out of the corner of my eye.

'Yes, she is, but relax, calm down. She won't take a bite out of you, you know.' Mairin laughed again and introduced me to a tall, good-looking girl called Olivia.

She wore a pretty, flowered dress, make-up and jewellery, so I felt safe again. I began to realise that my reaction to Marjorie was all out of proportion. Soon I was feeling really sophisticated at the idea of mixing with lesbians and not being a bit prejudiced. Wait till I tell Kathy, I thought, and wondered if there were any more at the party.

'By the way, Olivia is lesbian too,' Mairín said sometime later in the evening.

'Gosh, you'd never know, would you?' I was amazed.

'No, indeed you'd never know. She behaves just like a real human being!' Mairín grinned wryly at me.

I felt a right eejit. Someone put on music and people started to dance. I sat and watched.

'Come on, Margaret, wriggle your bones,' called Olivia. I got up and joined them, but felt a bit foolish dancing without a man. There didn't seem to be much point to it.

'Come on, Margaret. Loosen up. You're allowed enjoy yourself,' Olivia encouraged me.

Someone turned the music louder. More people got up and I felt less prominent. I started to move a bit more with the music, just dancing for the sake of dancing. It was the first time I'd done that since I used to practise tap-dancing in front of my parents' mirror when I was small. I was surprised at how enjoyable it was.

As the night went on, I noticed that Mairín was drinking rather a lot. She danced wildly around, giving the odd whoop or two, and occasionally reeling against the furniture.

'Mairín seems to be enjoying herself,' Olivia remarked. 'I'm glad to see her let herself go. She's far too serious and works far too hard. She needs a break.'

But Mairín just got drunker and drunker until, at two in the morning, I found her sprawled in a corner bawling her eyes out. Fran, Harriet and some others were sitting round her, trying to console her.

'Maybe we should get her home to bed,' I suggested.

'Could you take her home?' Fran asked me. 'You live beside her, don't you?'

'Not any longer. She's moved into her own flat, but I could go home that way easily enough.'

Between us we got her up, put on her coat, found her handbag and lifted her down the stairs to my car. She was a ton weight. On the way home she started crying again.

'Not one of them gives a damn for me, not one, not a single one,' she gulped. 'They don't give a shit. I work my guts out for them and all they do is take, take, take.' She burst into fresh sobs. I didn't know what to say. 'Do you care about me, Margaret?'

'Why, yes, I do.' I answered, rather embarrassed.

'Really and truly. Tell me the truth. Do you really give a damn about me?'

'Of course I do,' I answered, patting her shoulder.

I had never brought a drunk home before, so it took me ages to get her up the steps and find the key to get the door open. I helped her into the living-room and dumped her on the sofa, then I went to the kitchen to see if I could find some coffee to sober her up.

'Don't go. Please don't go,' she sobbed.

'It's OK, Mairín, I'm only going to the kitchen,' I assured her, thinking that I could do with some coffee myself.

When I came back with the coffee on a tray I found her lifting a bottle of pills to her mouth, trying to swallow them down. Oh my God, she's trying suicide, I thought in panic.

'Stop that!' I called to her in alarm, dumping the tray hurriedly on the floor. I jumped over to her and knocked the bottle out of her hand. The pills scattered all over the floor and she began to cry again.

'There's no point in going on,' she sobbed, 'nobody loves me, nobody at all.'

'Oh, don't be silly,' I said, in a kind nanny voice that sounded stupid to me, 'of course people love you.'

'Do you?' she asked, looking at me, her face all streaked and blotchy.

'Yes, of course I do,' I assured her briskly, the patient nanny with a fretting child. 'Now, come along and drink up your coffee, that's a good girl.'

'Do you really love me, though?'

'Yes, yes of course.'

'Then put your arms round me and give me a hug.'

What else could I do? I put my arm around her and she leaned on me. When she had calmed down a bit I gave her the coffee and watched while she drank it. 'Come on now, Mairín, I think you should go to bed,' I said firmly, and helped her into the bedroom.

She was still very unsteady on her feet. I didn't know if she'd be able to get undressed and into bed without help, and yet I felt rather embarrassed about taking off her clothes. However, the thought that she might have another bottle of pills somewhere convinced me that I should stay and make sure she got to sleep. I helped her out of her clothes, into her nightie and tucked her into bed. When she seemed to be breathing regularly I tiptoed out of the room.

'You're not going now,' she wailed after me, 'stay, please stay, please, please, please. Look, you can sleep here beside me. The bed is big enough, please.'

I didn't know what to do, but she sounded so piteous and

again the bottle of pills loomed up in my imagination. I would never forgive myself if she committed suicide. I got in beside her in my slip. After a short time she seemed to fall asleep. I was awake a good while longer, before I fell into an uneasy doze. Then I had a dream. I dreamed that I was in bed with a man who was caressing me. Suddenly, I realised that it wasn't a dream at all. It was real. I couldn't work out how I had got into bed with a man without knowing it. I lay there motionless, trying to work it out, and the caressing continued. Who is it? I thought frantically. Who could it be? Where am I? And then I remembered where I was. It wasn't a man. It was Mairín! For what seemed like an hour, I was paralysed, while a voice in my head screamed: 'What'll I do? What'll I do? What'll I do?' Then I could move again. I grabbed her hand roughly and pushed it away from me.

'Mairín, stop that. Do you know what you're doing?' I said, and half sat up to look at her.

She seemed to be asleep. Not an eyelid flickered. Her breathing was deep and even. Maybe she had been doing it in her sleep. I just did not know. I decided to give her the benefit of the doubt, but I didn't sleep very well after that. I kept jerking awake, feeling apprehensive, but nothing more happened and at last it was light enough for me to get up.

It was a quarter-to-seven and Mairín was still fast asleep. I dressed quietly and slipped out of the bedroom. As I was making for the front door, I remembered the pills and went into the living room to pick them off the carpet. I collected them on hands and knees in a saucer and poured them back into the bottle. I decided that I'd better take the bottle away with me, just in case. 'The Tablets', the label read, 'take one four times a day after meals'. They could have been anything.

When I got home I went straight to bed to try and make up for the night's lack of sleep, but I couldn't get what had happened out of my head. I kept wondering had she really been as drunk as she seemed? Was she serious about the tablets? Was she really asleep when she made those passes at me? But all the wondering in the world gave me no answers, only kept me awake. I began to wonder what would have happened if I hadn't stopped her. How much farther would she have gone? I was kind of sorry that I had stopped her so soon. It might have been interesting to see what it was like. Then a thought struck me. Maybe I'm a lesbian and I never knew it. A latent lesbian, isn't that what they call it? Perhaps that's why I'm still a virgin. Maybe it is nothing to do with my upbringing, and the fear of getting pregnant, and the lack of suitable men. Well, there is only one way to find out. I'll just have to find a man I like and go to bed with him. Whatever else, I have to find out.

*   *   *

5

OVER THE NEXT months Oliver continued to tell me about his previous girlfriends, but the only one I felt jealous of was the Japanese girl. I always sensed he was comparing me unfavourably with her. My resentment of her helped me to stick to my decision not to touch him unless he made the first approach. I wasn't sure whether he noticed or not. Certainly he said nothing. Worse still, he did nothing.

Each evening he came home from work, kissed me lightly on the cheek and told me what a dreadful day he had had. We ate, watched television and went to bed. He read the papers and I lay there totting up my grievances and rehearsing what I'd say to him when I got the chance.

The first grievance was that he made all the decisions about the house. It made me feel like a lodger. It was his house, his furniture, his kitchen, his bathroom, even his bed; and I was just his girlfriend, a piece of walkie-talkie furniture. And then he didn't even listen properly to me. He'd listen to the first bit and dismiss it with, 'You're too emotional, Margaret . . . . You're far too sensitive, Margaret . . . . Let's be sensible about this, Margaret . . . . Why can't you be more logical about this, Margaret?' Why can't a woman be more like a man, Professor Oliver Higgins? But, of course, he expected me to listen and smooth the fevered brow when he was emotional or feeling sensitive.

And the worst, the very worst thing, was that he never told me the things he appreciated about me, even though I was always careful to praise him, tell him the things I liked about him. No, that wasn't the worst. The worst was that he never told me he loved me. Sometimes when we made love I told him that I loved him, but all he ever did was hold me tighter and say, 'Oh

Margaret, Margaret.'

A million times I was on the point of asking him if he loved me, but at the last moment I always drew back. I thought it sounded so silly and dependent for a liberated woman like myself. Besides, I didn't want to pressure him. But if I was being really honest with myself, I knew I didn't ask him because I was afraid that the answer would be no.

In the beginning, he had said that our relationship would be a 'no strings attached' one. I had gone along with that, thinking that, given a little time, he'd change his mind and we'd get married. As I lay there totting up my grievances I was beginning to believe that nothing was going to change. I don't think he loves me, I thought unhappily, and if he doesn't love me I cannot go on living with him. I decided to give it another three months. Surely by then he'd realise and do something.

It took another three weeks of tea and television and fuming silently in bed before anything happened.

'How about going away for the weekend, Margaret?' he asked, coming up behind and putting his arms round me as I was doing some washing at the sink.

'Yes, that would be lovely,' I answered with a spurt of hope shooting up inside me. 'Where to?'

'I thought we might go to Sligo to see my mother.'

His mother! Irishmen don't introduce their girlfriends to their mothers lightly. It must mean something. Marriage maybe, but I dismissed the thought as too much to hope for, though it must mean some sort of change in our relationship. 'Oh Oliver,' I turned and put my arms round his neck and kissed him, 'that would be wonderful.'

'Watch out,' he said, 'I don't want suds dripping on my suit.'

This was what I had been waiting for. Everything would be grand from now on. Now I could forgive him anything.

Even in school things improved. Sister Magdalen was speaking normally to me and asked for my opinion about some change she was thinking of making in the timetable.

'Oliver and I are going away for the weekend,' I told Kathy.

'Lucky you. We're too busy saving up. Between the wedding and the new house, we're skint,' she replied. 'Where are you going?'

'To visit his mother in Sligo.'

'What's this, what's this?' she exclaimed. 'Is there something I should know about?'

'How do you mean?' I grinned.

'Come on, Margaret. It isn't every day that a man brings you to meet his mother. Are you thinking about getting married?'

'Don't be ridiculous Kathy,' I dismissed her, but secretly I was delighted that she had echoed my thoughts exactly.

The road west out of Dublin was crowded with commuter traffic on Friday evening. We were bumper to bumper, almost all the way to Maynooth, and Oliver was getting restive. Even when we'd left the suburban traffic behind us and were out on the open road the traffic was still heavy with country boys and girls returning home for the weekend. Oliver hated being delayed behind slow drivers.

'Christ, what an idiot!' he growled, frowning and compressing his lips as he passed a Volkswagen.

It was a hairsbreath, heart-stopping overtake in the face of an articulated truck. I closed my eyes, held my breath and pressed hard where the brake would be if I were driving.

'Relax, Margaret, relax,' he laughed. 'I know what I'm doing.'

'But Oliver, that was a very close shave. You shouldn't take those kind of risks.'

'They're calculated risks, Mag. That's the difference between you and me. You're a good driver all right, but you'd never get anywhere in a rally. You wouldn't be prepared to take the necessary risks. That's why you're in a nice, safe job, and I have my own business.'

I didn't point out to him that he'd never been in a car rally in his life. And anyway, I had come to live with him, and that was a risk, wasn't it? Sometimes Oliver could be very condescending. However, I decided that it would probably only start a row if I said that now.

'I was thinking that we could stay in Jim King's place tonight.'

'Who's Jim King?' I asked.

'Ah, he's a guy I knew back in the States. He's home here a couple of years now and he's got a hotel on Lough Allen. It's geared for wealthy fishermen and he's making a bomb.'

'Are you sure he'll have room for us if he's doing so well?'

'Course he will. Amn't I a friend? Anyway, I was talking to him during the week and I fixed it up with him.'

For the next couple of miles I wondered worriedly if I could afford a hotel aimed at wealthy fishermen. I never knew what to do about paying in these circumstances. Oliver used to complain about women who took it for granted that men would foot the bill, gold-diggers or inadequates he called them. At the same time he nearly had a fit if we were out somewhere and I tried to pay. It was very awkward. I thought we'd be staying with his mother and I had a gift all wrapped up for her in my suitcase.

It was dark when we arrived at the hotel, but even in the dark I could see the wide expanse of the lake gleaming, a lovely setting for a hotel. It had been a large Georgian mansion, and from the moment you stepped inside the door, you had the impression that you were being entertained by a gracious family in their gracious home. No wonder it was a success.

A very attractive and charming young woman registered us and brought us to our room.

'Mr King said that he'll join you later. He's away just at the moment.' She went over and drew the heavy gold curtains.

'Oh, Oliver. This is magnificent,' I said, looking round at the antique furniture, 'but it's going to cost the earth.'

'No, don't worry, Mag. It won't cost us anything. Jim owes me one.'

Well, that was a relief. We went down to the dining-room and, as we waited to be served, Oliver went through the menu estimating the real cost against the listed price of every item and working out the annual profit. The dining-room was full of the rich fishermen and a few fisherwomen.

'At these prices,' he confided, 'Jim's doing very nicely for himself. Nice little business.'

I was wearing a dress which Oliver had once told me was very sexy. I wasn't interested in Jim's profit margin. I slipped my hand over his and squeezed gently.

'Hey, you're looking great tonight,' he said and squeezed back.

This was more like the Oliver I had left home to live with.

By the time coffee and liqueurs came I felt that all the old intimacy was back again and Jim had to come and spoil it.

'Oliver, how are you?' he called across the dining-room and came over to join us. 'You must be Margaret,' he said, turning to me, 'so what do you think of the Cincinnatti Casanova, eh? That's what we used to call him back in the States, the Cincinnatti Casanova.' He turned back to Oliver. 'Well, how's the boy? Come on out to the bar and let's have a few drinks for old time's sake.

Together we trooped out of the dining-room.

'You know, this guy's amazing,' Jim said when we were all seated on the leather chairs in the bar. 'He always has a good-looking woman with him, and so far he has escaped marrying. You'll have to do something about that, Margaret.' He raised his glass to me and drank.

Oliver sat there and smiled enigmatically.

Obviously Jim now felt that he'd fulfilled his duty as a host to me and he proceeded to talk to Oliver about people they had known in America, about business deals that had been done, and business deals in which he was now involved. It was all very boring and I was getting tired. We'd had a long drive after a day's work. I wanted to go to bed, but Oliver looked all set to go on talking for hours.

'I think I'll go on up to bed, if you don't mind,' I said, politely stifling a yawn. I'd be better off watching television than being bored out of my mind by a conversation from which I was totally excluded. I hoped that Oliver would take the hint.

I lay in bed looking at an undistinguished black-and-white Ealing Studios' film, feeling badly done by, but I reminded myself that it wasn't really Oliver's fault. He couldn't very well run away from his friend, especially when we were staying for free in his hotel.

The film had almost ended when Oliver arrived with a bottle of champagne in one hand and two glasses in the other. 'Sorry for the delay, but I'm thinking of starting a business in the west and Jim is a useful contact.' He put the bottle and glasses down carefully on the bedside table and took me in his arms. 'Jim says I don't pay you enough attention,' he murmured.

'Oh, Oliver.'

'He thinks you're terrific, you know.'

I held my breath, feeling sure that he was going to add how he felt about me.

'Hey, I brought champagne. Let's open it,' was all he added.

I let my breath go. You could die that way.

We sat in bed drinking and giggling and Oliver made love to me the way he had done that first weekend in Wexford.

'Oh Oliver, I do love you,' I said when it was over and we lay there, tangled and sweaty.

'We can't sleep together in my mother's house, you know,' was all he answered. Then he yawned, turned over and fell asleep.

'I love you, I love you,' I whispered to his back, and wondered who I was trying to convince. Was Oliver really any different now than when I first met him?

*   *   *

The telephone rang and my mother answered it.

'It's for you, as usual,' she said, 'Mairín Weldon.'

I wondered what I'd say to her. I hadn't seen her for a week since the party, and I felt so embarrassed about everything that had happened. I lifted the phone nervously.

'Margaret? My God, was I dreadful the night of the party?' she asked, and continued without giving me a chance to answer, 'I was out of my mind. You know, I don't remember the half of it. I don't think I've ever been so drunk in all my life. Thanks a million for bringing me home. Was I absolutely awful?'

'Well, you were fairly mouldy all right.'

'God, don't I know. I shouldn't have been drinking at all. I was on antibiotics for my sinus and I was warned not to mix them with alcohol, but you know how it is at parties.'

'Oh well, don't worry about it,' I said.

'Look, Margaret, I want you to do something for me. How would you like to go on television for Women Together?'

'Well, I don't know. I'm not sure. Why me?' Shouldn't you be going? What's it all about anyway?'

'The *Monday Debate* programme is doing this thing about women and they want us to send someone along. I can't go because I'll be away on holidays that week, chatting up handsome Spaniards in the sun.'

'But surely there's somebody else who could do it. After all I'm not all that long in the group.'

'There's nobody else who could do it without having a nervous breakdown on the screen.'

'But I've never been on television before. I don't know a thing about it,' I protested, half-pleased at the prospect, half-frightened.

'I know, Margaret, but you're a teacher. You're used to standing up there in front of people, talking.'

'Talking to a class of children is not quite the same as being on national television,' I protested, but eventually I agreed to do it; her remark about chatting up the handsome Spaniards made me feel that she was telling the truth when she said that she didn't remember what had happened when I brought her home from the party.

Before Mairín went on holidays she, Fran, and Harriet coached me on what I was to say. I wrote it all down and wondered how on earth they expected me to get all that across. *Monday Debate* was usually a panel discussion so I'd probably only get a minute or two.

When I arrived at the studios I was met by a thin young man in faded jeans, who carried a clipboard and looked as though he had far more important things to do. He introduced me vaguely to two men who were in the waiting area. I recognised one as the psychiatrist who was always brought along when anything vaguely psychological was discussed on television. The other was a good-looking priest. They smiled. I smiled, and we talked about the weather for a few minutes. Then a well-known woman agony-columnist came in, exclaimed delightedly at the psychiatrist and gave him the very latest news about a mutual friend. I was left talking to the priest.

'Are you going to be on this programme about women?' I asked.

'Yes, indeed I am,' he chuckled, as though it were all a huge joke. 'I have a special interest in the role of women in the Church, you know.'

'I'm glad the Church is at last taking an interest in women,' I said mildly.

'Oh, I can see we have a pretty radical lady here.' He chuckled again.

'Well, the Church has shown little interest to date,' I said, feeling rather irritated by his manner. 'I don't think that's exactly a wildly radical view, just a matter of fact.'

'I can see I won't get away with too much with you around.' He laughed and patted my knee as though I were a small child who has made an unexpectedly clever point.

I was absolutely furious with him, but I drew a deep breath and decided that this wasn't the place to deal with him.

The door opened and Marion Foster came in. She was a well-known journalist, whom everyone either hated or loved because of her forthright views. I read her column religiously every Saturday and thought she was great. She was very tall and wore a dramatic mixture of reds and glitter. I would have given my eye teeth to have had the nerve to dress like that. Her long earrings caught the light as she greeted our group and said hello to the television people she knew.

The young man with the clipboard reappeared and herded us to the make-up room.

'I suppose you're nervous,' he said.

'Yes, I am,' I smiled nervously back.

Marion overheard the conversation and turned to me. 'There's no need to be nervous,' she said. 'Most of the people watching are only putting in time till the *News*, sports, or *Dallas* comes on. They'll be half-asleep anyway.'

The man with the clipboard sniffed as though he had been personally insulted and moved away from us.

'It's the interviewer who's responsible, and he'll help you out because if he doesn't it's a lousy show and his reputation is at stake.' She grinned encouragingly at me. Put like that it sounded much easier. 'Television people', she added in a low voice, 'are so convinced that everything they put on screen is of world-shattering importance that they expect the rest of us to be awed by it. I wouldn't give them the satisfaction of saying I'm nervous – '

'Is this your first time on television?' asked the make-up girl.

'Yes, it is.'

'I suppose you're very nervous?' she said sympathetically.

'Well, no actually, I'm not,' I answered, with as much conviction as I could.

I caught Marion's eye in the mirror and she gave me a huge wink and a thumbs up sign.

The hospitality room was crowded. Someone came round and introduced himself as the producer, smiled briefly, asked me if I was nervous, and moved on.

'Most of these are the lads looking for free booze,' Marion said in my ear.

The producer called for attention. There was a small man at his side whose face I recognised. It was Joe Finlay, the presenter of *Monday Debate*. I had always thought that he was about six foot tall.

'Joe here will tell you about the show,' the producer said.

Joe smiled and looked modest. 'Right,' he began, 'you all know the format. We're on the air at eight-thirty, commercial break round eight-forty-five or -six, depending on the discussion, and finish at three minutes to nine. There will be a studio audience, and as you know I'll invite them to comment, but you are the people I'll concentrate on.' He smiled round at us with dazzling dental work and humorous eye-crinkles. 'I have a few things in mind for the discussion. You know, the usual stuff about women's liberation. How far has it come? What more changes are needed? Is women's role changing? The role of the Church. You know, that kind of thing. I'll ask each of you questions, but if there's something you want to say, feel free to say it at any time. That's what this programme is all about, letting people express their opinions.'

'Are we going to have a rehearsal?' asked the agony aunty.

'You'll all get a chance to do some talking when we're doing the voice levels, but I don't want to rehearse too much. I like to keep the discussion fresh.' He flashed us another eye-crinkler and went to the door to shout to somebody.

The rest of us went back to our drinks.

The producer came in again. 'OK, everybody,' he called, 'voice levels and positions. We'll take you one at a time.'

'You'd think they were preparing for open-heart surgery in there,' Marion remarked to me when she returned.

I knew what she meant when I went in. Bearded men in jeans were moving cameras round and peering into them with earnest frowns. A man in a three-piece navy suit held headphones on his head and gabbled urgently into a microphone to someone called Sam. Joe Finlay had his jacket off and a clipboard in his hand and was busy giving instructions to a cameraman. They made changes in the script. A kindly person in a thick-knit aran pullover clipped a microphone to me and urged me to relax in the tones of a nurse about to give an injection.

Finally, Joe noticed that I was there and came over smiling. 'Let me see, you must be Mairín, Mairín Weldon, isn't that right?'

'No. Mairín was unable to come. I thought you were told about that. I'm Margaret McCabe.'

'Oh yes. I have it here. OK, Margaret, you're representing Women Together. Right Paddy,' he called to someone, 'ready for voice levels?'

'Right,' a voice called back.

He crinkled intimately at me, looking deep into my eyes. 'Margaret, you represent Women Together, a feminist group. How do you think things have changed for women in the last ten years?'

I had only said a sentence and a half when he put his hand up and said, 'Hold it, Margaret. That's fine, great, terrific. Thanks a lot, Margaret!' He went over to the producer and the kindly man in the aran sweater, unhooked the microphone again and led me across the cables, round the cameras and back to hospitality.

There tension was mounting. Studio people were calling things to one another in television back-room-boys' language. The panelists were smiling nervously and wondering if they should go for a final pee. The free loaders were consoling themselves with drinks and telling stories of famous people who were a bundle of nerves before they went on the small screen.

'OK, folks, you're on. We're ready now,' the producer called, rubbing his hands. We were shepherded into the studio, warned not to trip over the cables and seated each side of a desk with 'Monday Debate' written in large, polystyrene letters. Joe Finlay was in his place, straightening his tie and nodding over to the man in the three-piece suit. The studio audience were settling down and gawking at the panel to see if there was anyone famous on it. I took a drink of water, because I felt as though my tongue was welded to the roof of my mouth. I was very nervous.

'Don't worry. It'll be all right,' Marion encouraged me, and I felt a bit better.

The priest leaned back, crossed his legs and beamed at the

better.

The girls were thrilled at the prospect of the outing. The days before were a frenzy of preparation. I got them to plan what they'd need to bring and I put Pat in charge of seeing that it was all organised. She had a wonderful time over that week, making out lists and bossing everyone around.

'Don't you think they need more supervision?' asked Sister Magdalen.

'I think it's good for them to take responsibility, Sister,' I found myself explaining anxiously. 'And actually I have been keeping an eye on things just in case.'

She pursed her lips and took a deep breath. 'Very well, obviously you know best.' Her tone implied that I deserved everything that was coming to me.

Damn her, damn her, damn her anyway, I thought. Why do I put up with it? She always makes me feel in the wrong, like a silly irresponsible schoolgirl. For the millionth time I remembered that it was just the way I used to feel when I was a Junior Girl and Sister Dominic gave out to me. What could she do to me? She couldn't fire me, after all I'm permanent; but then you never know with her, she is so well known and highly thought of that maybe she could; certainly she could drop delicate hints to the school inspectors that I am unsuitable or difficult and make staying on in St Brigid's very uncomfortable. But you're not a Junior Girl now, I reminded myself, you should have grown out of that by now. You're an adult woman, there's no reason to feel inadequate. But no matter what I told myself the feeling remained.

On the Friday before the outing Oliver got up and started to pack a weekend case. 'I've decided to go to London this afternoon,' he announced. 'Seeing as how you won't be here, I thought I might as well go over and visit my brother.' Like Sister Magdalen, he didn't look at me but concentrated on folding a shirt instead.

'Oh I see,' I said brightly, 'well that's grand then.' But I felt a great thunk of disappointment. From time to time he had talked about the possibility of the two of us going to London together, and now he had decided to go alone. I'd never met any of his family either and I was curious. I always had the feeling that if he audience. The psychiatrist leaned forward, put his head to one side and looked serious.

'Ready to go now,' someone shouted from the shadows.

'Good luck everyone,' called the producer.

The theme music swelled up through the silence and we could see the titles on the monitors.

Joe straightened his shoulders as the music faded, looked earnestly into the cameras, and said, 'Good evening, and welcome once again to *Monday Debate*. I'm Joe Finlay, and this evening we'll be talking about women. Has liberation done anything for Irish women? How has liberation affected women in the home, women at work, women in the Church, women's image of themselves? These are just some of the things we will talk about tonight on *Monday Debate*.'

There was another swell of theme music. Joe introduced each of us and gave us a chance to say something meaningless and innocuous about women's liberation.

Then he turned to the priest. 'Can you tell us, Father, about the work you've been doing?'

'I've been asked to help in looking at women's role in the Church,' the priest said smoothly. 'We are looking at ways of making better use of women's special qualities, their caring, gentleness, and of course their special role as mothers, which the Church has always reverenced in the person of Our Blessed Lady, the Mother of God –'

'What about our strength, our courage and our spirituality?' Marion interrupted. 'Don't you think they are virtues which your Church could use too?'

'Well, of course,' he answered suavely. 'Yes, indeed, we are most anxious that women be given a fuller role in the Church.'

'Does this mean that we're going to have women priests?' I found myself asking.

'Oh no, no, no,' he laughed indulgently. 'I don't think we're quite ready for that yet –'

'Well we are,' said Marion.

'Now ladies, festinare lente,' he waved an admonitory hand at us, 'we must hasten slowly in these things.'

'Two thousand years seems a slow enough hasten to me.' Again I spoke without even thinking. 'It's about time now for the

Church to let women into its power structure.' Oh God, I thought, what have I said, and the whole country watching?

Anyway, it got the audience going. Everyone wanted to say something. It seemed as though the debate was really only getting going properly when it was three minutes to nine and the programme was over.

'Great programme, Joe,' called the producer. 'Great programme everyone, thanks.'

I could hear all the television people echo 'Great programme' to one another.

'I didn't think it was all that great. It didn't deal with anything,' I said to Marion on the way out.

'No, they never really deal with anything, but as long as they get a good row going they're happy. I loved the way you got to that priest. He was so revoltingly condescending.'

'You weren't doing too badly yourself.'

'Let's go for a drink and celebrate.'

I got a very mixed reaction to my first ever television appearance. Women Together on the whole approved, but some of them, Harriet in particular, didn't think I said enough about the organisation. 'You should show more respect for a minister of God,' my mother said sadly, 'priests are only human, and you should have shown more respect.' My father said nothing at all, which meant that he disapproved so much that he wasn't even going to argue with me. 'I believe there is some anti-clericalism amongst the staff,' Sister Magdalen remarked to Kathy when I was within hearing distance, and proceeded to ignore me for the next few weeks. 'Fair do's to you, you're a gas woman!' Nora Harvey said, and Geraldine agreed. Everyone else wanted to know what Joe Finlay was like and were suitably amazed when I revealed that he was not the six-footer he seemed. 'Come on out with Tom and me for a drink tonight to celebrate,' Kathy had said.

And that's how I met Oliver.

Tom, Kathy and I were sitting in the pub having a drink when a voice called. 'Tom, it's Tom McCarthy, isn't it? It's a long time since I saw you. How are you anyway?'

Tom looked around to see who it was. 'Oliver Fitzgerald!' he exclaimed. 'Well if it isn't the oul' divil himself. Where have you popped out of?'

Tom introduced Kathy and myself and they got to talking. They had been to school together in Sligo and when Tom went to the University in Dublin, Oliver had gone to America. He had been only eighteen then, and now he was hoping to return and set up a business here.

'Didn't I see you on television last night?' Oliver said, looking at me closely.

'Yes, you did,' I smiled, thrilled that I had been recognised.

'I thought so. You're the one who took on the priest. It's about time somebody took those bastards on. They've been making our lives a misery for far too long. You know, I like a woman who stands up for herself.'

He gave me a long, appraising look, and I could feel myself blush. He had to go soon after that and I was disappointed, because he seemed rather nice and I was sure I'd noticed a something in his eye that showed he was interested.

Next day, just after the mid-morning break, Sister Magdalen came into my classroom, looked at a spot on the wall, and told me icily that there was a very urgent phonecall for me, and perhaps I should take it. Normally there was no question of a teacher receiving a call during class time. I wondered what on earth it could be. Maybe something had happened to my parents. I lifted the receiver apprehensively.

'Hi, Margaret. This is Oliver. Remember we met last night?'

Of course I remembered. 'Oh, hello,' I said, quite flustered by the unexpectedness of it.

'You don't sound too glad to hear from me.'

'No, no, it's not that,' I hastened to assure him. 'It's just that I wondered how you found out where I am?'

'Well you did mention that you worked in a special school. I looked up the phone book and rang every one till I found you.'

'Oh.' I was dumbfounded.

'I've been talking to some silly bitch who didn't want to let you take the call, so I just told her it was a family emergency.'

'That was my Principal, Sister Magdalen,' I giggled.

'Besides, it is an emergency. I have to go back to the States at the end of the week and I want to see you before I go. Are you free either tonight or tomorrow?'

Of course I'd be free, but I didn't want to sound too eager. 'I'm not free tonight,' I lied, 'but I could make it tomorrow.'

'Great. So how about I pick you up round seven-thirty and we can go someplace and have dinner?'

'Terrific, but you needn't come to pick me up. It's too far out and difficult to find. I have a car. I'll meet you in town. Would your hotel be OK?' I didn't want him coming to the house where my parents would meet him and get that when-are-you-two-going-to-get-married look on their faces.

'Fine, tomorrow, seven-thirty at the Burlington. I'm looking forward to it.'

So was I. There weren't many Irishmen I knew who would go to all that much trouble to make a date. It just went to prove what Kathy and I always said, they need to be deported for ten or twenty years to learn how they should treat a woman.

Sister Magdalen was standing at the end of the corridor with a snooty expression, looking at her watch. 'Is everything all right at home, Miss McCabe?'

'I think it's going to be all right. Just a family matter.' I smiled and had to clamp my teeth together to stop myself from making up some overblown story to convince her that the call was a genuine emergency.

'Family matter,' she repeated, and didn't sound a bit convinced.

I was too delighted that Oliver had rung to feel even the slightest twinge of guilt.

The restaurant was all discreet service, stiff white napery and glinting silverware. The waiters materialised when needed and evaporated when we'd been served, like genii out of a bottle. It must be costing a fortune I thought. Oliver insisted on champagne and even though I don't like it very much, I sloshed it back enthusiastically. He even presented me with a rose. Mind you, it was the rose out of the table decoration, but still, it was a very romantic gesture.

Throughout the meal he told me how interesting and attractive I was. He recognised that I was a very liberated lady and that was the only kind of woman he had any time for. He hoped that he would see a *lot* more of me when he came back permanently from the States next spring. My head was reeling with the compliments and champagne.

He also told me a lot about himself. After he had left Sligo, he had travelled all over the U.S., working at all sorts of things, until he decided to start a business of his own. He owned a couple of wholesale bargain-furniture stores there, but when he had sold them and returned, he thought he'd go into the dry-cleaning business, and had his eye on one or two likely places. 'I'm a country boy at heart,' he declared, 'I've no ties in the States, and I've always had a yen to come home.'

He didn't try to get me to bed. He just kissed me gently and held me in his arms. 'Oh yes,' he murmured, 'I want to see an awful lot more of you.'

As I drove home I was grinning idiotically from ear to ear.

Between then and Easter he telephoned me every week. On Valentine's Day he sent a huge bunch of flowers by Interflora.

'They must be from an admirer,' my mother said, obviously hoping to learn more, but discreetly not asking.

'They are,' I replied, Sphinx-like, not about to give anything away.

But I knew she must suspect something. She had answered the phone a number of times when Oliver rang and knew he was ringing from the States.

'Margaret, I'll be over at last for Easter,' he said the next time he rang. 'Why don't we go away for the weekend?'

'Oh gosh, yes, oh well . . .' I was taken aback at the suddenness of the suggestion.

'I'll be arriving in Shannon earlier that week, but I have to go to Sligo first. I'll be in Dublin late on Friday. Maybe we could set off first thing on Saturday. Why don't you arrange the hotel?'

'Yes. Yes of course,' I agreed, but my mind was in a whirl. Obviously, if I went away with him it meant sleeping with him, and I didn't know if I wanted to, at least I thought I probably did, but he didn't know I was a virgin, and what about contraception, and I hoped my mother hadn't heard the arrangement I was making.

'I'm looking forward very much to coming home,' Oliver said, 'and to seeing you again.'

Ah, he really was a very nice man.

I telephoned Kathy immediately and told her I needed to talk to her urgently, but not on the phone because my parents might overhear.

Ten minutes later I was banging her knocker.

'What's the matter?' she asked, while I was still on the doorstep. 'You sounded desperate.'

'Oliver rang and he wants me to go away with him for Easter.'

'Hey, that's great.' She saw the look on my face. 'Margaret, you are going, aren't you?'

'Well, that's the problem, Kathy. I don't know what to do. It'll probably mean sleeping with him.'

'I don't think there's any probably about it,' Kathy grinned.

'But, Kath, he doesn't know that I'm still a virgin.'

'That's simple. You'll just have to tell him. He probably won't believe it – hey, Margaret, you're not thinking of backing out now, are you?'

'Oh, I don't know . . .'

'Now, Margaret. You are thirty-four years of age. You're not exactly a child. You're not planning on going back to God unopened are you? I'd hate to think of my good friend dying wondering.'

I laughed at that. 'I suppose you're right.'

'Oliver is a very nice guy. I think you'd be mad not to. And don't forget to do something about it before you go. A little trip to the family planning clinic is called for.'

God yes. That was something else I'd have to think about.

I found it almost impossible to get myself round to making the hotel booking. I looked at all the ads for Easter holiday weekends, and decided on one in Wexford, but I still couldn't get the courage to lift the phone and ring. I told myself that I couldn't phone from home in case my parents overheard and I couldn't phone from school in case Sister Magdalen was listening on another line. Besides, it seemed so cold-blooded, planning on losing my virginity like this. I felt uncomfortably that it was something which should be done on a wave of passion, not planned in advance.

Finally, with Kathy's encouragement I made the call, but when the receptionist asked for the name I panicked. What name should I give? Eventually I stumbled out Oliver's name, because

I didn't have the nerve to say Mr and Mrs Fitzgerald, and I was suddenly sure that if I gave my own name someone I knew would find out and know what I was planning. 'And make it twin beds, please,' I added at the end. I was sure the receptionist knew, but the twin beds seemed to take the harm out of it. Besides, it gave me the feeling that I could still change my mind. I sighed, envying the heroines in American novels who lost their virginity with consummate ease to football captains – always it seemed in the backs of cars at drive-in movies.

It was Kathy who harrangued and plagued me till I at last made an appointment with the clinic the week before Oliver was due. I sat in the waiting-room, buried deep in a copy of *Time* and giving the odd, furtive glance round in case I saw anyone I knew. They put me on the pill, but I couldn't start it till my next period and that was after Easter. It was a relief really. It meant I didn't have to make a decision yet. All I'd have to do was tell Oliver that I didn't have any protection.

I told my parents that I'd be going away for Easter with Kathy, and went over to her house to plan what I'd wear for the weekend. I wanted to look my best.

'Take my poncho,' she offered.

'Oh, Kathy, I couldn't,' I protested, 'it's too good.' I had often admired the beautifully woven pattern and secretly thought that it looked much better on me than on her.

'No, go on. Take it. It looks great on you, and, after all, I was wearing your dress when I met Tom. One good turn . . .'

I gratefully borrowed the poncho. It would be much nicer than my old, green coat. But I didn't tell her about the pill, or the twin beds.

I picked up Oliver at his hotel on Holy Saturday morning. We drove out of the city, towards Wicklow. It was a brilliant spring day and the heat of the sun shining through the windscreen made it feel like summer. We drove down to Kilmacanogue and over wide, flat Calary bog. The mountains surrounded the brown bog in blue and lavender.

I pushed all thoughts of sex to the back of my mind. I'd think about it at lunch time, I told myself. I'd talk to him then about it. For the moment, it was delightful to be driving along with the man I probably loved. At my age, I thought, it is much easier to be sure of the kind of man you want. No wonder so many young marriages go on the rocks. They're far too immature to know what they really want. I drew a sigh of infinite wisdom.

'What's the big sigh about?' asked Oliver.

'Oh, just that it's a nice day and I'm enjoying myself,' I replied airily. I had no intention of admitting that I'd been thinking about marrying him.

'Definitely, this is the only country to be in!' Oliver sighed and settled himself lower in the seat. 'You know, often when I was in America, I used to imagine myself sitting in a sloping field looking out at the sea.'

I immediately added rich, green grass and hawthorn, flowering in cataracts, to the image. I smiled, thinking how poetic he was.

We stopped for a while on a high, bare mountain above a pine forest. The sweep of bracken, brown and burnt orange, flared with patches of gorse. Farther away the green appliqué patchwork of fields led the eye to a hazy sea. Birds swooped and dived in the light wind. The sun made spangles on the brown bog pool just below us. We held hands and gazed. Heaven!

I could feel a fart coming on and held it back. It was so embarrassing at a time like this. It seemed like some shameful malfunction of my body, like sweaty hands or bad breath. I moved away from Oliver briefly as though to a better vantage point, and covered my fart with a cough.

Near Aughavanagh we found an ideal place for a picnic lunch, a sunny clearing in a wood near a stream. We fed one another with sausages and toasted one another with wine. The stream swirled round rocks and chortled over stones. Sun slanted through the trees, creating a cathedral effect. A man and his collie drove a small flock of sheep along the road. He lifted his finger to his cap in greeting. I didn't think it was the opportune moment to talk to Oliver about the fact that I'd done nothing about contraception. Nor about the twin beds I'd booked in the hotel. No, later, later.

As we had taken our time and chosen the long route, it was late afternoon before we got to Wexford. We drove through the narrow little streets and out on to the Rosslare road. The Sliabh Dubh Hotel was a low, concrete and glass building. It had an overweight, abstract sculpture on the lawn. I parked on the tarmac outside a smoke-glass-walled corridor. Oliver took the baggage, while I collected Kathy's poncho from the back seat and made sure the doors were locked.

The entrance to the hotel was through a heavy, revolving glass door with a chrome push-bar. I passed through this into the open foyer. There were my parents sitting in the whooshy, simulated-leather chairs, drinking tea! In front of them was a tray on a low table. I stopped short. The next section of the door hit me in the back. My first thought was, they hate tea in places like this, and immediately, Jesus Christ, what am I going to do? For an instant I was paralysed. Then, without thinking, I pushed the door round and completed the full circle. Whew, I was in the open air again. 'What am I going to do?' I panicked out loud. I tried to stand to the side, where my parents couldn't see me, and catch Oliver's eye. I could see him looking towards the door and turning back to the receptionist.

Then I remembered the poncho. I knew my parents had never seen it. If I put it on, perhaps I could slip across the foyer to the Ladies without being seen by them. So disguised, I went into the lobby, my back to the seats, walking crabwise, as though I were lost in admiration of the copper figures of Celtic heroes on the opposite wall. I tried to catch Oliver's attention as I passed, but he was deep in conversation with the receptionist. I was too anxious to get under cover to go over to him. I shot into the Ladies as fast as I could. As the door closed, I could hear Oliver call my name. Immediately I was inside, I realised that at any moment my mother could come through the door. I should have stayed outside the hotel. Oliver would have come out eventually to look for me. I slipped into the loo, bolted the door and sat down. Somebody came and used one of the cubicles. The toilet flushed. The taps ran. I heard a cough, and knew it wasn't my mother. Someone else came in, and then another. How long was I going to have to wait? How was I going to get out? Maybe I should send Oliver a note with one of the toilet flushers. I could say I felt sick and couldn't stagger out myself. I tore a page from my diary and wrote. 'The couple drinking tea are my parents!!!!! Let me know when they're gone.' I found myself giggling hysterically.

The door opened again and I heard my mother's voice call, 'Margaret?'

I froze. She must have seen me. Complex explanations of why I was here with a man instead of being in Cork with Kathy went through my head.

'Is there anybody here called Margaret?' she asked tentatively.

I suddenly realised, from the tone of her voice, that she was addressing a stranger in embarrassing circumstances. I had a brilliant idea. 'Yes,' I called back, in my best imitation of an American accent.

'Your husband wants to know if you're all right.'

'I gotta cramp,' I mumbled.

'Are you all right?'

'Sure. I'm fine. I'll be out soon.'

She went to the toilet and then washed her hands. It seemed to take hours. I was convinced that she'd bend down to look under the door and recognise my shoes. It was strange listening to all the little sounds that were so evocative of her. The way she clicked her handbag, the scuffle of her feet on the floor. I found that I was holding my breath. At last she went out.

I tore another page from my diary and wrote: 'That was my mother you sent looking for me!!!! Let me know when she's gone. Mag.' I waited for somebody else to come in. When I heard the next woman washing her hands I peeped out the door and, sure that it wasn't my mother back for another round at the taps, I slipped cautiously out. She wore a turquoise uniform, which must mean she was staff. 'Would you mind giving this to Mr Oliver Fitzgerald. He's the tall man in the foyer with the curly hair and glasses. I'm not feeling very well and I'm going to have to . . .' I gestured feebly at the toilet.

'Certainly,' she smiled. 'Are you sure you'll be all right?'

'Yes, yes. I'll be all right,' I shot back into the cubicle, smiling insanely.

After what seemed like a year's solitary confinement I heard the door open again. Nobody came in, but I heard Oliver's voice calling softly.

'Margaret? They're gone now.'

'Are you sure?' I called back, opening the cubicle door.

'Sure I'm sure. I can see them driving away.'

I came out into the reception area warily. 'Thank God they never stay in hotels,' I shuddered. 'They always stay in bed and breakfast places when they go away.'

'Hey, you're all up in a heap, Mag,' Oliver laughed. 'Surely you're old enough to do as you wish. Your parents couldn't possibly expect you to be still a virgin.'

'But I am,' I wailed.

He laughed again. 'Sometimes, Margaret, you're a scream.'

We went over to the reception desk where Oliver had left the suitcases. The girl I'd given the note to was behind the desk.

'Feeling better?' she asked, with a lift of her eyebrow and a knowing smile.

I was sure she had read the note and knew about my parents. I was also sure that she was scrutinising the rings on my left hand. I had a jumble of rings in the hope that I'd give the impression that there was a marriage band amongst them. I wanted to get away and up to our room as soon as possible.

At first, I only felt relief when I got to the bedroom and closed the door. Then I began to feel uncomfortable. I still hadn't told Oliver about not having any contraceptives. Anyhow, now I wasn't so sure that I wanted to let him make love to me. At the same time though, I wished he'd just sweep me off my feet so that I didn't have to make any more decisions about it. I fussed round the room, hanging up my clothes, carefully placing my toothbrush and paste in the bathroom, arranging my comb in front of the mirror.

Oliver took one look around. 'These bloody, modern hotels never have double beds,' he exclaimed, pushing the twin divans together. I said nothing, happy that he thought the twin beds were the hotel's fault. He came up behind me and kissed the back of my neck. His hands came round and caressed my breasts. I lay back against him and closed my eyes. He turned me round and kised me full on the mouh.

'Oliver,' I whispered, during the breathing spaces. 'It's true what I told you downstairs.'

'Mmmmmm,' he answered, not taking any notice.

'I really am a virgin.'

That stopped him for a moment. He drew back from me and looked quizzical. Something about me must have convinced him. 'I'll be very gentle,' he smiled, and continued kissing me.

'But Oliver, I haven't any . . . I mean I didn't get, you know . . . anything . . .' I began to protest faintly.

'Don't worry, Mag, I've brought some.' He showed me the packet.

I lost my virginity without further ado, and with considerable pleasure. Afterwards I lay there thinking. I didn't even mind that I was lying on the hard bit between the two beds.

'Oliver?'

'Mmmmmm?'

'I wonder why they talk about "losing" your virginity?'

'Mmmmmm.'

'Because really it's like gaining something, isn't it?'

I was ready for a discussion about the matter. Oliver was asleep.

When he woke up we made love again. I wondered what on earth had prevented me from doing this years ago. It was so much fun.

Soon it was time to go and eat. Before we left I checked both of us carefully. I didn't want anything in our appearance to suggest what we had just been up to. We were excessively neat as we stepped out of our room.

The hotel was offering a special candlelight dinner. I wasn't too sure what was so special about it, except that there was a three-piece band playing romantic music. I was surprised to find I was mildly shocked. Holy Saturday was always a day of polishing and cleaning at home, the last day of Lent with a night of religious services. I felt quite guilty as the veal *cordon bleu* was placed in front of me. Oliver wound his leg round mine. We touched hands, smiled knowingly, kissed between mouthfuls, and gazed at one another over our wine glasses. I knew that we were in love. The waiter didn't bat an eyelid. He'd seen it all before. Somehow his expression suggested a cynically raised eyebrow to me. I made sure that my ambiguously ringed hand was out of view when he was around.

Later, couples started dancing on the square of parquet in the centre of the room. That really would be romantic, I thought.

'Come on, let's dance,' I suggested.

Oliver wasn't too keen, but after a bit of persuasion he got up.

We moved slowly, cheek to cheek. I had never before danced with somebody knowing that I was going to go to bed with him. It was quite different from usual. Normally, I held myself ready to push away, to turn my head to an inaccessible angle, to use all sorts of subtle hand pressures to indicate that I wasn't available to anyone who was coming on too strong. This time I didn't have to. I melted into Oliver's arms as languidly as any heroine in a novel.

'Margaret, please, remember we're in public,' Oliver whispered urgently. 'You'll make a disgrace of me on the dance floor.'

He shifted away from me slightly. I wished he'd whisper romantic things in my ear. We danced on in silence and I nibbled his ear occasionally. I wanted to make love again, but I didn't like to suggest it. I put a finger through his shirt front and tickled his chest.

'Come on, I know what you want,' he said, removing my hand from his chest. 'I'd better get you to bed or you'll make a complete disgrace of me.'

'Oh yes, please,' I grinned.

'You'll have me killed before you're finished.'

He laughed and I took it that he was only joking. Men always talked about sex to me as though they were insatiable. I assumed that Oliver must be the same.

*   *   *

Now as I lay listening to the sounds of the lake outside I knew that Oliver was no Casanova. I noticed the half-empty bottle of champagne and wondered if he would want to finish it in the morning.

6

MRS FITZGERALD lived in one of those bleak, grey, two-storied, slate-roofed houses that you see all over the west of Ireland. It stood in a bare yard surrounded by a dry-stone wall with a couple of twisted thorn trees to one side. Its sashed windows looked blank and it had its back turned resolutely to the Atlantic. All around were magnificent views, Ben Bulben, the Ox Mountains and, far away, the wild coast of Donegal. But the bent thorns and the grey house ignored the grandeur.

We drove up a pot-holed *boreen* from the main road. As we turned into the yard, Mrs Fitzgerald came out of the door, wiping her hands on a towel. She wore a blue nylon overall and pushed back a streel of grey hair as she bent, frowning, to see who was in the car.

Apprehension leaped like a cat and sat on my chest. 'She is expecting us, isn't she?' I asked Oliver before he opened the door.

'No. This is a surprise visit,' he said, and got out of the car.

'Will ye look who's here!' she exclaimed as he went over and kissed her on the cheek. Immediately she ducked her head round his shoulder to watch me.

I joined them and stood smiling, hoping I was making a good impression as Oliver introduced us.

'What a magnificent place to live in,' I said when we had shaken hands politely.

''Tis surely, lovely altogether,' she replied. 'I suppose it's nice for visitors, but you'd want to try it in winter with a shower of hail coming down from the north. Ah 'tis bleak enough then, I can tell you.' She gave me a slow, appraising look. I was glad that at least I wasn't wearing high heels. 'Coleman's gone to town for a part for the tractor,' she said to Oliver, moving towards the house. I knew that Coleman was the eldest brother, who ran the farm. He too, was unmarried and lived in the family home with his mother. The other brothers and sisters were scattered from Vancouver to Wembley.

'When'll he be back?' Oliver asked as we entered the kitchen.

'He should be back any minute now. Will ye have a cup of tea?'

'Yes, please, that would be lovely.' I smiled. 'Can I give you a hand, Mrs Fitzgerald?'

'Not at all child, not at all. Sit down there and rest yourself.' She indicated the worn armchair at the side of the Aga cooker. 'I suppose it's from Dublin you are?' she began her inquisition.

'Yes I am,' I replied, knowing that would be a mark against me, 'but my parents are from the country.'

'What on earth brought them to Dublin? It's a very noisy, bothersome, dirty place. I've been there a few times, but I couldn't stand all the traffic and the rush. What took them there at all?'

'My mother went there to do nursing. My father was in the Civil Service. They met and got married, so I suppose that was that.'

I knew the information she was looking for and I could see that she was satisfied with what she had learned, but slightly despising that she had got it so easily. It would take a lot more time and guile to learn as much about her business.

'And what is it you do yourself?'

'I'm a teacher. I work at a special school with children from deprived backgrounds.'

'Well now. That must be very interesting.'

Mrs Fitzgerald came from a tradition which considered land and money a far sounder basis for marriage than compatability or love. Being a teacher was as good as money in the bank. You could work after you were married. The job was permanent, and you got a pension. I could see my stock rising visibly.

She patted me on the shoulder and handed me a cup of tea. 'Drink that up now,' she said. 'I have some sweet biscuits here in the tin, if Coleman didn't eat them all on me.'

Oliver had told me that his family had a good farm, not magnificent, but comfortable. His father had drained land and availed of agricultural grants long before the Common Market was ever heard of. The prosperity showed in the huge colour television in the corner, the spacious fridge and the deep freeze, but nobody had inveseted much in décor. The kitchen had been painted a virulent turquoise and had a neon light in the centre of the ceiling. Over the Aga there was the inevitable picture of the Sacred Heart and an electric bulb with a filament in the shape of a cross burning in front of it.

Later Coleman came in. He was her unmarried son and worked the farm. He looked very like Oliver, but ruddier and more solid. The room suddenly seemed a lot fuller when he arrived. He wore a donkey jacket and wellington boots. When he was introduced to me, he wiped his hands along the legs of his trousers, took off his knitted cap and grasped my hand as though it was the hoof of a skittish calf he was trying to dose. 'How are ye doin'?' he grinned and nodded, and put his cap back on. Then he and Oliver went out to the yard, leaving the women together.

'Of course, Oliver is very good at doing for himself,' Mrs Fitzgerald said, as we were getting the evening meal ready. 'He learned all that fancy cooking in America, you know. I suppose it's as well for a lad to be able to feed himself when he hasn't got a wife.' She looked at me sharply as she said it. I was cutting bread and arranging it on a plate. 'You'd want to cut a deal more bread than that,' she said, 'there's two men to be fed.' But she must have approved of the way I laid the table and wet the tea while she was cooking the rashers and eggs because, just as we were ready to call the men, she said confidentially, 'Sure we'll make a farmer's wife out of you yet!'

After supper was over we sat round the table talking. They talked about the other members of the family; about the old doctor's drinking; about the nerve of the parish priest to stand up last Sunday and ask for more money, and he knowing the state the country was in; about the neighbour's cattle; about the great new job Mick Glynn's eldest got. I didn't know any of the people they talked about, but it was all part of Oliver's background that I knew very little about, so I enjoyed listening. Mrs Fitzgerald even got out some old photographs. There was one of Oliver just before he left school. He looked so open and innocent that I felt a surge of emotion for the man who was once that boy.

'I like this one of you,' I said, showing him the snap.

He smiled and found my leg under the table and pressed his knee against it. I slipped off my shoe and rubbed my toes up and down the inside of his leg. I felt really happy here with Oliver and his mother and brother in the house where he'd grown up.

'Mam, have you still got those old class photos we used to have taken every year in school?' Oliver asked.

'Of course I still have them,' she said, looking up from some old sepia-coloured print. 'They're inside in the good room, in the top drawer of the sideboard.'

Oliver went to look for them, and it was only when he had gone out the door that I realised that his leg was still there pressing mine. Oh no, it must have been Coleman all the time! I snatched my leg away and looked over at him, embarrassed and furious. He grinned and winked.

'Here's one of your Uncle Bertie,' Mrs Fitzgerald said, oblivious, 'I wonder now when that was taken?'

Coleman tried to hold my gaze and I didn't know what to do. I got up and went towards the door.

'Where's the eh . . . ?' I said, trying to sound natural.

'Oh, it's upstairs, straight ahead,' said Mrs Fitzgerald.

Coleman had turned towards me from the table. He had tilted his chair back a bit. His hands were behind his head and his legs were wide apart. He kept grinning idiotically at me. I got out as quickly as I could. I was mortified.

By the time I got back to the room the three of them were engrossed in the school pictures and exclaiming over the people they knew.

'Will you look at the Disco Kid!' said Coleman, pointing to a scrawny youth, with his hair standing up at the back. 'He's doing all right for himself with that disco of his.'

'I didn't know he was in that business,' said Oliver, alert for any useful information.

'Isn't that why they call him the Disco Kid. He wears a white suit these days, and I hear he's managing some band or other as well.'

'You know, I think I'd like to meet him again,' said Oliver.

'He's always in the disco of a Saturday night. Why don't you and Margaret come along and we could have a bit of a dance while we're there.' As he said this, Coleman looked directly at me and gave me a knowing wink. I looked away, pointedly.

'Why not?' said Oliver. 'We can go for a few jars first and then go on to the disco.'

'I suppose you'll be staying the night?' asked his mother.

'Where else would I stay?' said Oliver.

'I'd best show Margaret where she's sleeping then.'

She brought me upstairs and showed me into a large room painted ice blue. There was an iron-framed bed in the middle, a huge, dark wardrobe and matching dressing table, and a sagging armchair. I looked out the window and saw the Atlantic turning rosy in the light of the setting sun.

Oliver seemed to know everybody in the crowded pub. I sat sipping my vodka and tonic, my eyes smarting from the smoke and my ears bombarded with all the noise. I tried to keep a pleasant expression on my face. All the time people were coming over to Oliver and having long conversations which I couldn't hear properly. The bits I did hear were about local characters and events. Everyone wanted to buy him drinks, because it was so long since they'd seen him. Now and then a man would nod at me, point to my glass and say, 'What are you having yourself?' I'd have been roaring drunk if I'd taken all the drink I was offered. None of them talked to me.

Coleman jostled his way back from the bar with the drinks he'd gone to buy. He put my drink down on the table crowded with glasses and ashtrays full of butts, gave Oliver his pint of Guinness and took a swig from his own. 'Push up in the bed there,' he said to me.

I squeezed a little closer to the woman next to me and made a little space for him to perch beside me. I was glad of his company.

He leaned over and said in my ear, 'I'll be looking out for a big, sexy woman like yourself tonight.' He winked broadly as he withdrew his face.

I smiled politely and looked over to Oliver, but he was listening to an old man with no teeth who was talking and laughing with one arthritic fist held to his mouth and a pint of Guinness grasped precariously in the other.

We didn't leave the pub till the barmen were shouting, 'Drink up, please, it's past the time. Come on now gentlemen, ladies, please.' Of course, there would have been no point in going to the disco earlier. Nobody would be there till the pubs closed.

'Mindy's' the pink neon sign flashed over the door. The entrance hall was small, but the mirrored walls gave it an illusion of space. There were two men in the hall. One was obviously the bouncer, a burly man in his fifties with his hair oiled and combed like Clark Gable. He was talking to a much younger man in a lightly soiled, white suit and a black open-necked shirt. His exposed chest had a tan and a gold medallion. This had to be the Disco Kid.

'Jack!'

'Oliver!'

They pumped hands and slapped backs for a while.

Coleman went on in – to search for his big, sexy woman, no doubt – and I stood there smiling, waiting to be introduced.

'Margaret, you've got to meet Jack Maher, the Disco Kid. I promise you, he's a gas man!'

Jack brought us in and ordered a bottle of wine.

The inside of Mindy's was lit entirely with pink light coming from somewhere near the floor.

'Like the lighting, Margaret?' Jack asked.

'It's a bit like being in a pink fishtank,' I said.

He threw back his head and laughed. 'Not just a pretty face, witty too. Christ, Fitzgerald, you always do well for yourself with the women.'

Oliver said nothing.

Once the wine had been poured, the two of them settled down to the inevitable local talk and business, from which I was excluded.

Although we were in the bar it was still very noisy. Through an archway I could see lights flashing and people dancing. I wanted to dance. I jigged around in my chair in time to the music, in the hope that Oliver would take the hint. I would like him to myself for a while. After all, we were supposed to be away on this weekend together, but all he was doing was talking business.

'Do you want to dance?' said a voice in my ear.

I turned and it was Coleman. There was no sign of Oliver moving. Why not, I thought. I might as well be enjoying myself.

And I hoped that it might make Oliver a bit jealous.

Coleman looked rather smart in his good clothes, but without the restraining influence of his cap his hair stood out from his head in wild curls. For a while we danced separately to the disco sound. Then the rhythm changed to a slow sentimental tune. Coleman moved closer; planting his hand firmly in the middle of my back, he drew me towards him. I kept my head at a sharp angle, to prevent him putting his cheek next to mine. He pulled me even closer. I put my hand on his chest to hold him off a bit. It didn't seem to worry him, he sang along with the music, in my ear. When the rhythm changed again Coleman shifted his grip. This time it felt as though he was clutching my spinal column in his fist.

'Groovey baby, grooooo-veeeeee!' he kept repeating like a mantra, while he ground his pelvis against mine in time to the music. Then he tried to kiss me.

'I think I'd better be getting back,' I said, struggling out of his wrestler's hold.

'Ah, stay for a while, Margaret, go on. They'll still be talking. Come on, stay.'

'I think I'd better be getting back to Oliver,' I said pointedly.

'Look,' he pleaded, 'I'm sorry if I upset you. I won't do anything, promise.'

'You didn't upset me, Coleman, but I would prefer to go back now.'

We returned to the table. Coleman had been right. Oliver and Jack were deep in conversation. Jack offered me some more wine and asked how I'd enjoyed the dance. Then, without waiting for an answer, he smiled, nodded and leaned over to say something into Oliver's ear. Whatever it was, Oliver burst out laughing, and I felt isolated. Coleman sat beside me and stared out at the dance floor.

'You don't have to stay here, Coleman,' I said, giving him a sisterly pat on the arm. 'I'm sure you want to be off chatting someone up.'

'Ah no, I've looked around and there's nobody here tonight.'

'Go on out of that! There must be someone here that you fancy.'

'There is.' He leaned forward, smiling, and grabbed my hand. 'You.'

'Don't be ridiculous, Coleman,' I laughed, pulling my hand away from him, but pleased too. Coleman was rather attractive really, I thought, and it was pretty audacious of him to try and steal his brother's girlfriend from under his nose. I liked the hard neck of it, but I turned away from him. I couldn't really do that to Oliver. 'Oliver,' I called above the din, and cutting across his conversation with Jack, 'dance with me, will you? I'd love a dance.'

'No. I don't feel like it,' he answered, 'but don't let me stop you. Go ahead and dance all you want. Why don't you dance with Coleman? He's a great man for the dancing.'

Well damn him anyway, I thought angrily, if he wants me to dance with Coleman, I will! 'Come on,' I said, taking Coleman's hand.

'Sure you don't mind, Oliver?'

'Not at all. Go ahead.' Oliver waved airily at us.

This time I didn't try to hold him off. This time we danced as close as possible, arms entwined, cheeks glued together with sweat. It served Oliver right. When we got back they were still talking. I was getting tired and I wanted to go home. I yawned pointedly and looked ostentatiously at my watch.

'I'll bring you home if you like, Margaret.' It was Coleman, still at my elbow.

'Are you thinking of going home soon?' I asked Oliver, ignoring Coleman's suggestion.

'I will in a minute. Just hang on there.' He turned his chair and talked urgently into Jack's ear. Jack kept nodding his head. At last Oliver got up slowly, still talking and punching Jack's shoulder to emphasise a point. 'Are you ready, Margaret?' He smiled and turning to Jack said, 'Sorry I have to go, but this woman will kill me if I don't take her home soon.'

I sat in the front of the car with my hand on Oliver's knee, just to let Coleman know whose girlfriend I was. Coleman sat in the back. He slipped his hand round the door side of my seat to stroke the back of my arm. I moved my arm forward to stop him and his hand slipped under it and he stroked my breast. I shifted sideways, twisted in the seat and made bright conversation so that he couldn't touch me.

Oliver drove and yawned and said, 'I'm knackered.'

The kitchen was warm and the light seemed blindingly bright after the dimness of the car.

'Tea anyone?' asked Coleman.

'I'm going on up,' Oliver said.

'Me too,' I added, and followed him up the stairs.

Outside my room he kissed me briefly and said goodnight.

'Come in for a minute, Oliver,' I whispered.

'No. Better not.'

'Please, just for a minute.'

'Shhhh, Margaret, no. Don't be crazy. My mother will hear us. She's probably still awake.'

'Afraid of your mammy?' I asked nastily.

'Don't be ridiculous. Of course I'm not afraid. It's just that she's very old-fashioned. Well, you heard her yourself today. She wouldn't understand.'

As I got undressed, I argued fiercely with him in my head. I knew perfectly well that we couldn't make love with his mother next door. That wasn't the point. He'd been ignoring me all night. The least he could do was hold me – stay for a few minutes – tell me it was all right. But no, he was too afraid of his mammy to even come into my room, the bastard. If the situation were reversed and it was my home and my mother and I did that, he'd tell me I was being immature, that I was behaving like a child. I could just hear him. 'You're an adult now, Margaret. Surely you're not worried about what your parents think.' I vowed to tackle him about it at the first possible opportunity.

Mrs Fitzgerald had filled a hot-water bottle and put it in the bed. It created a small island of warmth in the cold bed. I thought the bed felt a bit damp. Probably nobody had slept in it for ages. It had a deep hollow in the centre and it took me a while to find a comfortable position, curled up with my back to the door. I lay there thinking about the way Oliver was treating me and wondering what I should do about it.

Then I heard the door open and Oliver whispered, 'Can I come in?'

So he'd changed his mind. Well, maybe he wasn't so bad after all, but I wasn't going to appear too delighted.

'Mmm huh,' I mumbled without moving.

I could hear the door close gently and him tiptoeing across the room. 'Hey, Margaret, you are awake, aren't you? It's me, Coleman.'

I struggled up out of the hollow. 'Oh. I thought it was Oliver.'

Before I had time to know what was happening, he was half into the bed, kissing me passionately. I struggled an elbow out from the blankets, and gave him a dig with it.

'Coleman, stop. Go away. Stop it this very minute,' I said in an urgent whisper. 'If you don't stop this very minute, I'll scream.' But even as I said it, I thought that it would serve Oliver right if I did let Coleman into my bed. Not that there'd be much comfort in this bed.

'All right, all right, I won't do anything. I promise. Just let me stay here for a while.' He sat up on the edge of the bed. 'Ooooh, you look very sexy, lying in bed there, Margaret.'

I didn't remind him that it was too dark to see much of anything.

'Give us a kiss,' he cajoled.

'No.'

'Ah go on, give us a birdie, please.'

'No.'

'Ah, go on Margaret, just one, that's all.'

'No, Coleman, no. I told you to go away, please.'

'Just one little kiss, go on.'

'No,' but I still let him stay there on my bed.

'Sure what's the harm in one kiss. I'll go after that, I promise.'

I didn't say yes, but then I didn't say no either, and he leaned over and brushed my lips gently once, twice and again, and then increased the pressure a little more and more until our tongues were entangled, and somehow his hands had got inside my nightie. Technically, I suppose it was still just one kiss. I didn't want to stop, but I knew that I should try to restrain his hands a bit.

'No, Coleman, no,' I gasped.

He ignored me and I let his hands go a little farther.

'No, Coleman. We've got to stop this.'

'Feel it, feel it,' he whispered hoarsely, grabbing my hand and putting it between his legs.

I knew it wasn't his clay pipe. I tried to pull my hand away.

'Oh, keep it there, keep it there,' he moaned, holding my wrist.

'No, Coleman, no!' I wrestled my hand back. The bed creaked. I was at a grave disadvantage being stuck in the hollow of the bed. Suddenly, I heard a noise outside. 'Hush, listen,' I whispered.

We both froze and listened. A door opened and footsteps came our way.

'Jesus, Mary and Joseph, it's me Mammy!' he exclaimed, looking wildly around. As the footsteps came nearer my door he rolled off the bed and under it. Suitcases must have been stored there, for something crashed against the iron bedstead.

There was a gentle knock on the door. 'Margaret, Margaret,' Mrs Fitzgerald called. 'Are you all right?' She put her head round the door.

'Yes, yes, of course,' I answered.

'I thought I heard something fall.'

I was sure she must be able to see her son lying under my bed, and I let the eiderdown fall casually over the edge to cover him. 'Yes,' I improvised, 'my handbag was on the bed. It must have fallen off when I turned over.' I could see it clearly on the dressing table, outlined against the window. Please God, don't let her notice it, I thought.

'Oh, that's all right then,' she said, and withdrew her head.

It must be my fate to get mixed up with parents every time I get involved in something sexual. Coleman rolled out from under the bed and brushed himself down. His mother went to the toilet. We waited in silence to hear her pulling the chain and pad back into her bedroom.

'Whew, that was a close one,' I said.

Coleman just stood there, trying to see over his shoulder to brush the dust off his back. I wanted him out before anything else happened.

'Well, good night,' he said, sheepishly and tiptoed out.

I tried drifting off to sleep, telling myself that it would be madness to start getting involved with Oliver's brother, but I found it difficult not to think about him. Sister Dominic in school would have called them bad thoughts. I remembered instead about the first weekend with Oliver.

*   *   *

When we'd finished breakfast that morning in Wexford, I put the tray on the floor and snuggled up to Oliver.

'Oh no, not again,' he groaned, 'come on, I think it's time for you to get up.'

He gave me a slap on the bottom and pushed me out of the bed. I was rather disconcerted. All I wanted was a cuddle. I dismissed the feeling as unimportant.

My thighs felt like I'd spent three days in the saddle. 'Gee, I'm sore,' I groaned, rubbing my thighs.

'I'm not surprised, the way you go at it,' said Oliver unsympathetically.

'Now I know why they call it riding,' I said.

'Margaret, please!'

I realised he was shocked.

Easter Sunday morning was warm. The sun was shining and the narrow streets of Wexford were chequered with light and shadow. We walked hand in hand on the sunny side, looking into windows and listening to passing conversations. Many of the shops were open and doing a brisk trade with the crowds coming from mass. Everyone was dressed in their Easter Sunday best.

Two men in brown suits leaned against a car and held a conversation with a friend who had just pulled up his van in the centre of the street. It was causing an obstruction, but nobody was worried. A woman in a car waiting behind let her children out. They ran into a sweet shop, clutching money. 'Look at that,' laughed Oliver, pointing to the traffic jam, 'you wouldn't get the like of that in America!' I wasn't sure if he was condoning or condemning. I laughed too, assuming that he was thinking that the scene was a wonderful example of how the Irish do not get fussed about time.

A men's outfitters had a yellow and red plastic sign which said: 'Mr Eager – Male Supremacy Starts Here'. Round the door there were bunches of wellingtons and oilskins. The windows displayed confirmation suits and donkey jackets.

'I suppose that's the level of liberation in this country!' smiled Oliver.

'For some,' I answered, feeling slightly miffed, as though he were criticising me.

We went into a deep, brown shop, full of shadows. At the end was a bar, just big enough for a pair of elbows and a couple of pints. A mahogany counter ran down each side of the shop. It sold everything from bread and matches to fertiliser and farm implements. Oliver loved it. He spent some time examining large paper sacks and an assortment of rakes and hoes. Then he went to the bar and tried to order a pint. Nobody came near him. The owner was too busy muttering serious-sounding things to an elderly man standing by a huge coil of hosepipe.

'That's what's wrong with this country,' exclaimed Oliver in irritation, 'if this was America we'd be served by now. But nobody here is interested in making money like that. They're far too easygoing.'

Farther down the street we came to a chemist and Oliver went in. I followed him. The shop was fairly full. An old man was buying elastoplast from the assistant. Two men were discussing liver fluke with the pharmacist. The old man left and a mother came in with a couple of children. Three teenagers were trying out lipsticks.

'Can I help you?' the fresh-faced assistant smiled at Oliver.

'Yes please. I'd like some Durex,' he said.

'Oh, Mr Maher deals with the veterinary things.'

I was too embarrassed to laugh. God, he should have more sense than to ask for condoms in an Irish chemist shop. Doesn't he know you can't get them just like that!

'Durex is not a veterinary product,' said Oliver evenly, 'I'd like two packs please.'

'I'm sorry, I'm not sure if we have them. Just a moment. Mr Maher,' she called, 'Mr Maher, this gentleman is looking for Durex. Do we have any?'

Mr Maher froze. The two farmers with the liver fluke problems concealed grins behind their knobbly hands. The mother sniffed. I became engrossed in a display of nappy liners. Mr Maher flapped his hands at his assistant.

'That's only on prescription,' he said in a tight voice, 'and anyway, we don't stock that sort of thing.'

'Sorry, we haven't any,' smiled the girl.

'On prescription!' Oliver started, but I pulled his sleeve and he came out into the street.

'But that's ridiculous, Margaret.'

'I know, I know.'

'That's absolutely crazy. Prescriptions for rubbers. That's just unbelievable. This country is not only primitive, it is absolutely lunatic.'

'You're right, you're right,' I agreed with him.

He was beginning to attract attention. I didn't think I could cope if somebody came over and started to abuse him for talking about filthy contraceptives on an Easter Sunday morning. I had a horrible feeling that my parents would appear and find me with this man who was haranguing the whole town of Wexford about rubbers. I willed him to quieten down and move away. At last he began to move from outside the chemist, but he continued to complain loudly about this country. In spite of all my campaigning for free access to contraceptives, on this my first practical experience of trying to get some, I was dying of embarrassment and afraid that somebody I knew would pass and find out.

'But I thought the law had been changed recently,' Oliver shot at me, as though it was all my fault.

'Yes, it has, but it's still very limited. You have to be married and go through a doctor before you can get anything. Of course, there are the family planning clinics, but I think they're illegal under the new law.'

'Jesus H. Christ!' was all he said.

By now we were outside a Catholic repository. The window was full of statues and holy pictures. Weak-chinned Sacred Hearts and strabismic St Josephs stood meekly together against a backdrop of china and plastic plaques bearing 'God Bless This House' or 'The Kitchen Prayer'. In the very centre of the display was a ten-inch high, gilt and plastic replica of St Peter's in Rome. A hand-written notice leaning on the dome said: 'Musical – Faith of Our Fathers'. Pictures of the last three pontiffs were glued to the windows. I couldn't help laughing. Oliver didn't think it was funny.

'Pope rules, OK,' he said sourly. 'You know, Margaret, I've only got one left.'

'Oh Oliver, it doesn't matter,' I said lightly, but I was a bit disappointed. We did have two whole days to go.

'At the rate you go it's not a bit all right. I hadn't expected you to be so enthusiastic, Margaret.'

He grinned. I grinned. Good humour was restored. I stopped feeling guilty about Irish law.

'Irish women make such a fuss about sex and then feel guilty when it's over. Pity they wouldn't take a few lessons from American girls.'

I was annoyed at the crack about American women. It was just what Kathy and I always said, Irish men always think the far away hills are greener. But then, maybe he did know what he was talking about. He had lived in America for years, after all. Anyway, I didn't feel a bit guilty.

'I suppose we could go to the seaside and walk along the strand for a while.'

'I suppose we'd better, in view of the condom shortage,' I quipped.

'Margaret, really!'

It was the second time that he sounded shocked. Maybe I was being a bit crude. I wouldn't have thought twice about it if it were Kathy, or even my brother Patrick, but that last thought didn't dawn on me for a long time afterwards.

We drove out to the seaside. The sand-dunes were hairy with sea-grass. The water was bright blue and whipped into little foam-topped waves by the wind. Sky and clouds were reflected on the wide, wet sands, like a sepia print. I jumped down the dunes to the flat sand and started to run. I wanted Oliver to run with me, but maybe I'd seen *Elvira Madigan* too many times. He walked purposefully along and told me about his plans for setting up a business in Ireland. He went into considerable detail.

I watched the tide sneak in as he talked. Sometimes it caught me unawares and sloshed over my shoes. Two horses galloped along the beach, their riders moving with them as though they were one. A man in a dark overcoat walked along swinging a walking stick, while his adventurous little dog snapped and barked and dashed into the waves. Some children were bent over the high-tide mark looking for shells and other treasures.

I found it difficult to concentrate on what Oliver was saying. Bank loans, suitable premises and machinery didn't interest me just then. There were far too many interesting things on the beach.

When we got back to the Sliabh Dubh Oliver said: 'I'm going to ask the hall porter for some rubbers.'

'How would he have them?' I asked in surprise.

'Oh Margaret, you are naive.' He shook his head at me. 'For the right money hotel porters can always get you anything.'

I decided that I'd go and have a bath while these negotiations were taking place, so I was hunting for the little green tablet of soap round the milky bath water when Oliver came back. He stood in the doorway. From his expression I realised that he was not thinking lasciviously of my body.

'Do you know what that cowboy down there charged me?'

I didn't think he needed an answer.

'Five pounds!' He waggled the packet at me.

'Is that expensive?' I asked, inadvisedly.

'Expensive!' he exploded. 'It's outrageous. It's highway robbery. Sometimes I wonder what brought me back to this country.'

I was beginning to feel that somehow it was all my fault again. I was only glad that I hadn't been there when he was buying them. I wondered idly if the fact that the rubbers were so expensive would make our lovemaking less enjoyable for him.

On Monday we went to Kennedy Memorial Park. We bought fruit and yoghurt for lunch. The picnic site was full of families enjoying the Easter sun. While we were eating, a little girl came over to us. Oliver started to chat to her, and soon she was offering him a piece of her Easter egg. Won't he make a wonderful father, I thought.

When we went to bed that night, I decided to do something that I had wanted to do all along: be sexually aggressive. I had been feeling a bit hesitant about it in case Oliver didn't like it. He seemed to like it a lot, except that he got so excited he took over when I wished he'd let me do it all. Soon he was ripping open the first of the expensive rubbers. It was difficult to get the foil opened and he grunted at it in impatience. Finally he got it open, put it on and leaped on me. About ten seconds later he jerked back his head, bared his teeth and moaned, 'Ooh, ow, ow, ow, ooh.' He raised himself up, arms rigid. I must be having an exceptional effect to have him moaning in passion like that. Up to now he had been quite silent in sex. He rolled over on his back and said through his teeth, 'Christ, this blasted thing is killing me, oowch.' I realised he was talking about the rubber and I burst out laughing. 'It's not bloody funny. I can't get it off. Do something can't you. Get me a scissors.' I ran into the bathroom to check my washbag. I wasn't sure if I'd brought one. I couldn't find it, so I picked up a razor blade of Oliver's and brought it in to him. 'Don't come near me with that,' he screamed in near hysteria. 'You could destroy me forever.' Then I remembered that I had a nail scissors in my handbag. I got it for him and he cut through the rubber and released himself. He lay there on the bed, groaning. Well, that's the end of that for tonight, I thought resignedly.

Next thing, Oliver was scrabbling at another packet. For a second or two I thought he had recovered his desire and my hopes rose briefly, but he just wanted to read what was on it.

'Made in Taiwan,' he read aloud. 'I've always heard that the Japanese have no sex drive. No wonder when they've such tiny little pricks.'

'Taiwan isn't Japan,' I said, in the interests of truth.

'It's as near as makes no difference,' he snapped back.

Later we lay in one another's arms. Oliver fell asleep with his head on my elbow. Just lying there asleep he looked so vulnerable, so innocent, just like a little boy, that I felt a great sweep of tenderness and I wanted to protect him, never let him be hurt.

I lay awake for a long time thinking about my life up to now, and of my future with Oliver. Well, now I knew I wasn't a lesbian. 'Liberated at last,' I sighed aloud to myself and smiled. I was getting pins and needles in my arm and the place where the beds met was getting harder and more uncomfortable under me, but I didn't like to move in case I should waken him.

'Hello there, Margaret,' said my mother as I came in with my weekend case, 'did you and Kathy have a nice time?'

The liberated feeling seeped away and I felt guilty. I avoided looking at her. 'Oh yeah, it was great. The weather was terrific. I suppose you spent all the time in the garden?' I said, knowing full well that she hadn't, but I thought her answer might give me a clue as to whether she had seen me in Wexford.

'No, no, the weather was so good that your father and I decided to go to Wexford. Your father thought he'd do some birdwatching. You're looking tired dear. Are you all right?'

'Yes, fine. We were out late at a party and met some people we knew and went back there for coffee,' I lied, feeling sure that she must know it wasn't true just from looking at me.

When watching TV my mother remarked disparagingly about performers whom she didn't like, that they had an 'experienced' look about them. I felt sure she could detect that look about me now. I was certain that my every movement betrayed the fact that I had spent the weekend in bed with a man. I thought the smell of sex must be oozing from every pore.

'You're looking a bit peaky, dear. It's a long old drive from West Cork. Maybe you should go to bed early.'

I went to my room and examined my face for giveaway signs. It didn't look any different from usual. Then I telephoned Kathy and arranged to meet her.

'Well, how did you get on?' she asked.

I told her about meeting my parents and she laughed herself silly.

'But you did sleep with him, didn't you?'

'Yes, yes, I did.'

'Well . . .?'

'It was great. I enjoyed it, but . . . I don't know, Kathy.'

'Why? What's wrong? Don't tell me you weren't using anything.'

'No, it's not that. It's just that I've got this guilty feeling. I feel certain my mother knows.'

Kathy threw back her head and laughed out loud. 'Margaret, don't be such an eejit. If your mother had seen you she'd be sure to say something. It's just the years of good convent education sneaking up on you. It gets you when you least expect it.'

'I suppose so.' Already I was beginning to feel better.

'So tell me, when are you seeing Oliver again?'

For the next couple of months I led a double life. Oliver had bought a house and was busy setting up his business. I often stayed with him at the weekends, telling my parents that Nora

Harvey had just got a cottage in the country and I was staying with her. They had never met Nora, so that was safe enough. Sometimes I said I was going to stay with Patrick and Helen. My brother and his wife knew about Oliver and encouraged me. It was hard on the nerves. Whoever said that a successful liar has to have a good memory was right. Sometimes Oliver and I made love during the week and I had to drag myself out of bed in the small hours and drive home. There were thirty-seven traffic lights between his house and mine. I entertained myself on the way home seeing how many lights I could get through before getting stuck at a red one. Once I got the whole way home on green, but mostly they were red.

'Margaret, why don't you come and live with me?' Oliver said after about six months of this, as we were lying on his king-size orthopaedic bed.

'Oh Oliver, I'd love to, but my folks would have a fit.'

'But we can't go on like this. It's ridiculous, you running off home in the middle of the night. I can't get a proper night's sleep.'

I immediately felt guilty for disturbing him. 'Look I'll think about it. It's just . . . well, I just know my parents will have a fit.'

'Come on Mag. I thought you were a liberated woman. Where are all your women's lib ideas now?'

That made me feel even guiltier because I'd almost given up going to the Women Together meetings since I'd met him, but instead I countered, 'That's all very well, but you don't know my parents.'

'Ah, don't worry. All parents are the same. They'll get over it in time. Besides,' he stroked my hair, 'you know how I feel about you.'

'No, Oliver, I don't. You've never told me,' I said, with my heart in my mouth with fear and anticipation of what he was about to say.

'You're very easy to have around. I love the way you take things so calmly, not like my last girlfriend. Christ could she scream! Of course her family's Italian.'

It wasn't exactly a passionate declaration, but it was the nearest he'd yet come to saying he loved me. For the moment I was satisfied. I thought about telling him I loved him, but decided it might be premature.

'It's two o'clock, Mag. You'd better be getting home,' he yawned, 'I've a heavy day tomorrow.'

I left obediently.

I talked to Kathy about leaving home. She was all for it, but then it was all very well for her. I talked to Mairín about it too, but I didn't say I was leaving to live with a man. I just told her I was leaving home. 'It's the most sensible thing you've ever done,' she declared. 'Anybody who continues to live at home is daft. You need to be independent. I'm only sorry I didn't do it years ago.'

The only one who fully understood my problem was Patrick. 'Look Margaret,' he said when I told him, 'has it ever struck you that Mam and Dad might be glad if you left?'

'No. How do you mean?'

'Well, they too have their lives to lead. They've reared their children and now they should be able to do what they like without having to worry about us. They've given us all a good education, so we're well able to look after ourselves.'

'There's no need for them to worry about me.'

'Margaret, listen. I know they needn't worry about you. You know it. But as long as you're living at home you're still the baby girl that needs protection no matter what age you are. If you were living somewhere else they wouldn't know what was going on, so they wouldn't worry.'

I hadn't thought of it quite like that before. But another snag hit me. 'Patrick, I'm not just moving out. I'm moving in with *Oliver.*'

He grinned. 'Well, you're a big girl now and they'll just have to get used to it.'

'I'm trying to figure out when would be the best time to tell them.'

'You might as well make up your mind that no time will be a good time. They're not going to like it, so you'd better just say it as directly as possible and as soon as you can.'

'You're right, I suppose,' I said dubiously.

'You can count on me for support anyway. They'll just have to get used to the fact that things have changed since their day. Come on Margaret, cheer up. In no time at all, they'll be congratulating themselves on being so liberal.'

I thought I'd tell my mother first. She'd at least listen without immediately blowing up. Mammy could break the news to Daddy. She would have ways of getting round him. It would be much better coming from her than from me. The only thing was that every time I was working myself up to saying something the phone would ring, or the Legion girls would call with *The Sacred Heart Messenger* or Mammy would launch off into some topic and I couldn't interrupt.

In the end I didn't have to tell them. They found out. I decided to stay with Oliver one week night and told my parents I'd be with Kathy and might stay overnight. Unfortunately I had lost my keys earlier that afternoon and had been in a bit of a panic because my classroom key was on the bunch. It had a name and address tag on it, so I was afraid it might be found and used in a break-in. After I left the house my father found my keys and phoned Ferguson's to reassure me that they were safe.

'Oh, she's not here. She's probably with Oliver,' Kathy answered, without thinking. She knew I used her as an excuse, but I hadn't mentioned it specially on this occasion.

'I'm sorry, Margaret. Really, I am very sorry,' she told me the next day. 'It was out of my mouth before I realised what I was saying. I could have bitten my tongue off.'

'What did he say?' I asked.

'Nothing. He just said, "I see", and put down the phone.'

Obviously my father had put two and two together and probably made four.

Mammy was doing the ironing when I got home from school. I came into the kitchen and she sighed and wiped away a tear. She hated ironing and always chose to do it when she was depressed.

'It'll kill your father, you know,' she said and sniffled.

I said nothing.

'You did stay the night with him, didn't you?' she asked, with a faint edge of hope to her voice.

'Yes.' It was out in the open now. All I could feel was relief. I might as well tell her everything. 'I'm thinking of moving out soon, because Oliver and I want to live together.' I felt amazingly calm as I said it. For the first time ever I was talking to her adult to adult.

'Oh, where did I go *wrong*?' she cried. 'I thought I did everything I could. I tried to bring you all up as good Catholics. I thought I was doing everything for the best. I knew not going to mass would lead to something like this.' She shook her head sadly over my father's best blue shirt.

'Look, Mam, you didn't go wrong. You did everything the right way. It's just that I am an adult, you know. I've been responsible for myself for the last sixteen years at least. People's ideas change in sixteen years. My ideas have changed. Nothing I do is your fault any more, Mam. Please try and understand that.' It was awful to see her being guilty about me.

'I know, I know, but I can't help feeling that if only I'd done things differently, maybe not have been so strict, it might have made a difference. I don't know what your father's going to say.'

'You don't have to tell him I'm leaving. I'll tell him myself,' I said, not feeling nearly as brave as I sounded.

When my father came in from work he took off his coat, folded his scarf and hung up his hat with great deliberation. He came straight to the point. 'Where were you last night young woman?'

I could see the muscles in his jaw working.

'I stayed with Oliver.'

'Did you now? So you lied to us about where you'd be staying.'

'I didn't think you'd understand, Daddy.'

'You're dead right I don't understand, and I don't intend to understand either.'

'Dad, I'm an adult, and I can do as I like.'

'Not while you're under my roof, you can't.'

'Well, that won't be for much longer. I'm going to live with Oliver.'

'You mean living in sin. Isn't that what you mean?'

I drew a deep breath and held on to my patience. 'I don't think it's a sin, Daddy.'

'Does your mother know about this? It'll kill your mother, you know, kill her.'

My mother came out of the kitchen with no visible signs of imminent death. 'Now Bernard, don't be upsetting yourself,' she said. 'Come on in and have your dinner. Margaret, look what you've done, upsetting your father like that.'

The next week was very uncomfortable, but I got through it.

Communication was reduced to sad reproaches and long sighs. My mother told me that I was killing my father, and my father assured me that it would be the death of my mother. Both seemed in excellent health. Oliver came to help me move my things and Dad gave him a long lecture on the sixth commandment. Oliver took it very well. I was afraid that they'd end up shouting at one another, but Oliver had the sense to stay quiet throughout the tirade. 'We're all entitled to our opinions, Mr McCabe,' he said evenly when Daddy seemed to be finished. 'Mine are different to yours.'

Mammy helped me to get things packed, but she didn't say much. When we had done almost everything, she brought me a small statue of Our Lady. 'I know you think this is all just superstition,' she said, 'but I'd like you to keep this statue. Do it for me please, Margaret, and I hope you'll be safe.' She gave me a quick hug, turned away and wiped a tear. I was near to tears myself. I'm leaving this house forever, I thought, and suddenly wanted to throw myself into my mother's arms and cry and cry, but Oliver and Daddy were breathing heavily at one another downstairs. I carried down my suitcases and started to load the car.

'You need never set foot in this house again, do you hear that!' my father shook his *Irish Independent* angrily at me.

'Don't be ridiculous, Bernard,' snapped my mother, coming downstairs with a box of books, 'of course she's welcome to come here any time she pleases. There's no need to be so Victorian. There have never been any splits in our family and we're not going to start now. You'll be up for lunch on Sunday, won't you Margaret?'

'See you Sunday,' I called as I drove away.

As Oliver carried the last plastic bag into my new home I sat down and burst into tears. I was crying for my lost home, the awful strain of the last week, the fear of really being on my own now. Oliver didn't know quite what to do with me.

'There, there,' he said. 'There's no need to cry. Dry up your tears, Margaret. That's a good girl.' He pushed a bunch of tissues at me and went out to make a cup of tea.

When it came I sipped weepily and thought that at least I had Oliver, so I wasn't completely alone. I felt a bit better. Later I got the energy to start unpacking; apart from clothes, I had little property except books and the souvenirs and curiosities I had brought home each year from Europe. Oliver told where me he'd like me to put them. Well after all, it was his house, wasn't it?

*   *   *

7

JUST OUTSIDE Sligo town fat raindrops began to hit the windscreen. They fell faster and faster as we travelled, until Oliver had to have the wipers going at full speed. The rain drummed noisily on the roof of the car and the radio poured out disco music and crackle. It would be impossible to discuss anything over that noise. Anyway, he'd only tell me to keep quiet because he had to concentrate. The rain and the dark did make driving difficult. It wouldn't be a good idea to have a row with him now. Besides, I needed time to think.

That morning he had actually gone to mass. To mass, no less. This was the guy who laughed and told me I was ridiculous when I said that sometimes I went because I didn't want to hurt my parents.

'Hurry up, Margaret. We're going to mass,' Oliver had said to me as I came down the stairs that morning.

'To mass?' I had asked, raising my eyebrows in surprise.

'Of course,' he replied. 'It's Sunday. We're all going to the eleven o'clock.'

Mrs Fitzgerald came down the stairs, pulling on her gloves. 'We'd better get going or we'll be late,' she said. 'We'll go in your car, Oliver. It's more comfortable than Coleman's.'

'Go on out of that, Ma,' Coleman joked her. 'You only want to show off the grand car your son back from America can afford.'

'Don't be silly. Oliver's car is more comfortable for my poor back, and a sight cleaner than yours. Hurry up now. We don't want to be late.'

I got into the back with Coleman, leaving his mother to sit in the front. I was thankful that she kept turning round to point out things to me. It meant that Coleman had to keep his hands off me, but it didn't stop him sitting as close as he could, and rubbing his thigh against mine. I was terrified that Mrs Fitzgerald would notice.

I suppose I could have refused to go as a matter of principle, but I didn't like to, when Oliver was going. It might embarrass him. Then too, his mother seemed to have taken to me and I didn't want to ruin it by not going to mass. She'd be sure that I was going to corrupt her son. However, at least when I was in the church I didn't answer the responses, not even when Mrs Fitzgerald passed me a missalette. As for Oliver, not only did he answer all the responses, he sang the hymns, and even went to communion as though he were doing it every day of his life. After all he had said about religion! It was the last straw, the final betrayal.

I felt the same as I had the time I met Eamonn Butler, the great atheist from college, in Grafton Street. His head was as byronic as ever, and he had his son by the hand. The boy had his father's good looks and curly hair, and was wearing a First Communion outfit. Eamonn started to explain before I said anything. 'We have to give them something,' he said. 'It's different when you have children. It never really did us any harm, now did it? I don't want him to feel left out in school. It'll give him something to rebel against,' etc., etc., etc. And then, to add insult to injury he added, 'Of course, I don't believe in all that stuff myself.' I felt disgusted. I had always admired Eamonn because I thought he was a man of principle. Up to that Sunday in Sligo, I thought Oliver was one too.

I watched the oncoming lights through the clear fan which the windscreen wipers made. The dark road sloshed by. Oliver occasionally leaned forward to adjust the radio. He changed stations without consulting me, but of course it was his bloody car and his bloody radio, and he was doing the bloody driving. He seemed quite unaware of how I was feeling as he casually cursed other drivers. Occasionally, he made a comment about his mother; about Coleman; about The Disco Kid. All the while I fumed and fumed and said nothing. At last I could stand it no longer.

'So who's not afraid of his mammy?' I burst out, without any explanation.

'What do you mean? What are you talking about?'

'You told me only last night that you weren't afraid of her, so why, then, did you go to mass this morning? Sudden conversion, was it?'

'You went to mass this morning too.'

'Yes, but I only went because you as good as ordered me to go, and I didn't want to embarrass you in front of your mother.'

'I never ordered you to go. You needn't have gone if you didn't want to.'

'But that's not the point, Oliver. You were always telling me how silly I was because I used to pretend to my parents that I went to church, and now you're doing exactly the same thing. And you say you're not afraid of your mother.'

'Margaret, you don't understand. It's different in the country. You just can't do anything you like there, you know. I told you, I'm thinking of starting a business in Sligo. I have to be seen at things, talk to people. I'd be expected to go to mass. They all know who I am down there. They're all neighbours, you know.'

'Funny thing,' I said sarcastically, 'there's a lot of neighbours round where I live too.'

'It's not the same in the city,' he said and lapsed into silence.

The radio crackled on, making it easier not to talk.

Next day Kathy wanted to know all about it. 'How did you get on with his mother?' she asked eagerly.

'Grand, I got on very well with her, but wait till I tell you. I think Oliver's brother fancies me!' I told her the bit about Coleman coming into my room, but left out the bit about Oliver ignoring me all the time. I had never told Kathy about any of my difficulties with Oliver. I felt sort of ashamed to mention them. I had told her about his cooking, and that he did the laundry and so forth. I would have liked to talk to her about the problem, but it seemed like admitting some kind of failure. Once I'd said it aloud, I could no longer pretend to myself and I'd have to do something about it. After the weekend though, the problems weren't as easy to ignore.

I was mulling over them when I went into town to look for something to wear to Kathy's wedding. Finally, after eighteen months of saving-up, she was getting married in August and had invited me to be her bridesmaid, so I had decided not to go away for the summer. Oliver wasn't going to take any holidays either, because he was too busy, he said. I was finding the school holidays gave me plenty of time to think about my situation.

'Hi, Margaret,' a voice interrupted my thoughts. 'Remember me?'

It was Marion Foster, whom I'd met the night of the television programme. I felt rather flattered that she should want to talk to me.

'Of course I remember you. I was just a bit preoccupied and didn't see you there.'

She was wearing a combination of yellows and oranges. Her hair was shining and springy. Her skin looked clear and she radiated exuberance. I felt drab and dull beside her and wished, once again, that I had the nerve to dress like that.

'Hey, would you like to go for a drink? I need one badly. I've just spent a harrassing hour with Adolf Hitler's brother in the Department of Posts and Telegraphs.'

'Don't talk to me about men,' I replied, 'I'm very anti-man myself at the moment.'

'To a hostelry without delay then,' she proclaimed. 'Tell me all about it,' and she led the way across the street.

I don't know what it was about her that made me tell her all about Oliver and the weekend. Maybe it was because she looked as though she was really interested, or maybe it was just because she was a good journalist and knew how to get people to talk. Anyway I told her everything.

'Have you said all of this to him?' she asked, when I'd finished.

'Not really. I have said one or two things, but he wouldn't listen.'

'But have you tried asking him for what you want?'

'Well I've certainly dropped enough hints, but you might as well be talking to the wall.'

'Ah come on, Margaret. The first thing that every woman should know about men is that they do not understand hints. You have to give it to them straight.'

'But you'd expect someone who's supposed to care about you to have some idea of what you want. I am living with the guy. He should know me by now. After all, I have a pretty good idea what he wants.'

'Unfortunately, that's not the way it works. First of all, it really is a bit unfair to expect somebody else to be able to read your mind, isn't it? Secondly, you have to remember that we're brought up to think of others all the time. That's one of our worst problems. We're so busy doing good unto others that we forget all about ourselves. Men are brought up to think of themselves first and expect women to look after them. There's no point sitting round complaining about it. We've just got to do something about it.' She took a swig of her drink and settled down to her theme. 'Look, this is how I see it. I think we women have to decide what it is we want in our lives, and get on with it. I think we have to make our wants and needs clear to our menfolk and just refuse point blank to fall into all the old roles and expectations they have for us. We have to be our own women, that's what liberation is all about. It's not complaining about society, or demanding that someone should change it. Society is you, me and the man next door. We're the ones that have to make the changes. And we have to do it every day in all the little things. Liberation will never be given to us. It's something we're just going to have to get out there and take.'

'It sounds amazing when you put it like that.'

'It is amazing. If we can liberate ourselves we will totally change society. That's why we frighten the socks off so many people, men and women. There's an awful lot of people who don't like taking any resposibility at all, especially not responsibility for themselves.'

'But Marion, changing yourself isn't all that easy.'

'Nobody said it was easy. It's not easy at all, but it sure is interesting.'

'Well, you've given me plenty to think about.'

'Oh dear, I did go on a bit, didn't I? But you know I get really pissed off with some of the radical feminists and left-wing revolutionaries who want to change the whole of society, but won't do anything to change themselves.'

'Maybe I'll try out that bit about asking straight instead of hinting.'

'Think of it this way. The worst he can do is say no.'

'Ha, the *worst* he can say is: "You're being emotional Margaret", and refuse to hear what I'm saying.'

'If that's the case, you're going to have to make a decision, aren't you? Either you accept it and live with it, or you leave.'

I went home that evening feeling hopeful. Everything she had said made sense. She had such a positive approach. I wished I was more like that. I spent the next couple of days thinking out what it was I wanted to ask Oliver straight. There were so many different things I wanted to say to him. I rehearsed and rehearsed, but it all got so complicated that I put it off for another while.

When September came I still had said nothing to Oliver. I was back in school again and there was more trouble with Sister Magdalen: I was secretary of our branch of the teachers' union and every time we had to write a letter to Sister Magdalen she took it as a personal insult, because I signed the letters she blamed me for their contents. In one letter we requested that she let us know in advance the dates of the holidays and free days. This had been a source of contention ever since I came to the school. She would never give us more than a couple of days notice of when the holidays would start. It seemed a fairly simple, reasonable request, but not to Sister Magdalen.

'You used to be so enthusiastic,' she said, after she had summoned me to her office, 'and now all you are interested in is when you get your holidays. Have you no dedication left?'

'Sister, I wrote on behalf of all the teachers, not just for myself,' I replied, holding on to my patience.

'What is it you have against me, Margaret?' she continued sadly, as though I had said nothing. 'What on earth is it that makes you write a letter like this?' She held up the letter with the union logo on top.

'Sister,' I sighed, 'I have nothing against you personally. I am secretary of the union and I wrote that letter at the request of all the members. That is all.'

'Trade unions are a breeding ground for communism,' she said darkly.

'Sister, if you want to discuss the letter from the union, I would like some of the other officials present.'

'You're destroying the lovely spirit of the school,' she answered, shaking her head sadly.

I was furious with her, but as usual, just gritted my teeth and said nothing.

By the end of October we finally got it settled, but Sister Magdalen would not speak to me. Regularly she walked up and down the corridor outside my classroom, peering in suspiciously, and she told two of the new teachers that she was very worried about me because she thought I was very disturbed.

While this was going on in school I didn't have the energy to think of dealing with Oliver. Things just dragged along: school, food, television, bed, school, food, television, bed. I wished I could talk to him about Sister Magdalen. I really needed a shoulder to cry on sometimes.

That's it, I finally decided one evening, that's the first thing I'm going to ask him for straight: I'm going to ask him to listen to me. So, our meal over, we were on the couch watching TV when I began. I could feel my heart thump as I talked myself into talking to him. I must have taken the breath to start the first sentence at least fifty times, but each time I lost the courage. I kept telling myself that it was ridiculous to feel like this, but I couldn't help it. Oliver just kept watching the television.

'Oliver, I need to talk to you,' I blurted out eventually. 'Sister Magdalen was getting at me again today, and I'd like to talk about it.'

'You shouldn't let her worry you, Margaret. If I let little things like that worry me, I'd be out of business long ago.' He got up and went out to the kitchen to look for an apple.

'But Oliver,' I continued, this time I was determined, 'you don't know what happened. This time I'd like you to *listen*. I mean to listen properly and not be hopping up and down for things.'

'OK, OK, OK,' he said, coming back to the sofa. 'I'm listening. What is it?'

With him sitting there, his arms folded and a martyred expression on his face, I hardly knew how to begin, but I wasn't going to lose the chance. I told him all about Sister Magdalen and her reaction to the letter.

'Is that all?' he asked, when I had stopped.

'That's just one of the things that happen.'

'Well, have you finished, or do you want to tell me more, because there's an interview with the Minister for Finance on television in about two minutes and I don't want to miss it.'

I sat beside him, choking with rage and listening to the Minister avoid questions with elegant loquacity. I recalled Marion's words that liberation was something each of us had to take for ourselves every day. I got up, turned off the television, and stood in front of it.

'What are you doing?' Oliver exclaimed. 'I was looking at that.'

'Oliver, tell me,' I challenged, 'which do you prefer, me or the television set?'

'Don't be ridiculous, Margaret. Come on, turn it on again. That's a very important interview.'

'Not till you answer my question, Oliver. Which do you prefer?'

'Will you please calm down and just tell me what this is all about? I mean, why the sudden outburst?'

'I'll tell you what it's all about. It's about the fact that any time you come home tired and fed up and in bad humour you expect me to listen to your troubles, make suggestions, and offer sympathy, and I'm only too happy to do that. But when I come home, feeling fed up, and want some sympathy, there is always something more important on the television. Oliver, I need sympathy too, but you never, never, ever listen.'

'Haven't I just been listening to you? Of course I listen.'

'No, you weren't. You were keeping quiet while I spoke, waiting for me to stop to turn on the telly. It's not the same thing you know. Normally you don't even do that much. You just interrupt and tell me I'm being emotional or something. Well, Oliver, it won't do. It just won't do. I'm fed up being treated like a piece of talking furniture.'

'I never said that.'

'No, but you act like it, all the time.'

'What am I supposed to do, tell me that!'

'Treat me like an intelligent human being, that's what.'

'But I know you're intelligent. Of course you're very intelligent. Nobody's debating that.'

'Why then is it that unless we're talking about you, you don't bother to listen. That weekend we went away to Sligo, you ignored me the whole time and only spoke to your friends. If it hadn't been for Coleman I could have dropped down dead, for all you cared.'

'But Margaret, I told you I had business to do.'

'Oh, that's not the point. Tell me, Oliver, do you care about me at all? Do you really give one hoot about me, or am I just handy to have around?'

'I've told you how I feel about you.'

'No, Oliver, you haven't. You've told me what your friends think about me, but you've never once told me how you feel.'

'What do you expect me to say? What am I supposed to do?' He threw out his hands in a gesture of helpless incomprehension. 'Do you expect some passionate declaration or something?'

'Why not?'

'Oh, come on, Margaret. You're being very emotional you know. This is not the time or the place.'

'When is the time? Because I need to know how you feel about me, about us, and I need to know now. Do you love me? Do you?' There, it was out now. I hadn't intended to ask that. It just slipped out.

'Oh, love, love, *love,* that's all women ever think about,' he threw up his arms in disgust.

'Oliver, do you love me?' I persisted. I was no longer angry. I simply wanted a straight answer.

'You know I don't believe in love,' he turned away from me.

'Does that mean no?'

'You're putting words in my mouth. You know I like you. I think you're a lovely girl. Didn't I ask you to come and live with me!'

'Yes, you did, and I came because I loved you.'

'Look Margaret, I just don't believe in all that emotional stuff. All I want is a quiet life, without all these demands. Why do women have to make these demands all the time?'

'Does that mean no?'

'You're trying to push me into saying something, and I won't be blackmailed.'

'Does that mean yes?'

'I'm not prepared to commit myself just like that.' He folded his arms over his chest and looked away.

'That's not good enough for me, I'm afraid.' I replied. Calmly, I switched on the television again and left the room.

Well, at least I now knew where I stood. Maybe if I'd put it differently, maybe if I hadn't lost my temper in the beginning . . . . Well, there was nothing I could do about it now. In a way I had known all along. I felt a bit of a fool for having put up with it. I knew I couldn't stay here any longer. I packed a weekend case with the immediate necessities and decided to stay with my parents till I found a place of my own.

'I'm leaving now, Oliver,' I said when I came down the stairs again. 'I'll call for the rest of my things as soon as possible.'

'If that's what you want to do,' he shrugged and I left him watching a handsome man persuade a cretinous woman that Omo washes brighter.

My parents were very understanding and didn't ask questions. I just said that I was no longer going to live with Oliver and would they mind if I stayed with them till I got a place of my own.

'Maybe it's as well,' said my mother consolingly, 'I never thought he was your type, anyway.'

When I called to collect my things Oliver was standing there, looking portentous.

'Margaret, let's settle this like adults,' he said. 'I'm sure everything can be solved if we talk about it calmly, not screaming the way you were the other night.'

'I did not scream, Oliver.'

'No matter. You were quite unreasonable. Now, just tell me exactly what it is that you want.'

'It's quite simple. I want to be loved.'

'Wait now, Margaret. Let's not have all this emotional stuff again.'

'Oliver, I'm afraid that it's just that awful, emotional thing: I want to be loved. What is so terrible about that?'

'Women,' he spat in disgust, 'you're all the same. I thought you were different. I thought you had some semblance of logic.'

'Actually, I'm very logical, and I also want to be loved. They're not incompatible you know. Now, if you don't mind, I'd better get my things.'

'I might find somebody who's prepared to take me the way I am,' he called up the stairs after me. 'What'll you do then?'

'Wish her luck,' I replied, delighted that I had thought of the retort on the spot and not three days later.

'Jesus Christ prereve me from women!' he shouted, and slammed the living-room door after him.

When I had everything collected and packed in my car the house looked no different. It just goes to show how much of an impression I made on his life, I thought, as I drove away.

It's nearly a year now since I left Oliver. Shortly afterwards I found a flat. It's strange and difficult being alone, but it's a good way of finding out about myself. The idea of being able to do exactly what I wanted was marvellous, but the reality was different. At first I found that I had too much time to myself and didn't know how to fill it. So I used to sit round feeling sorry for myself and wishing Oliver would change his mind. I used to imagine that in one blinding flash he would realise how mean and uncaring he had been to me, that he'd come back, tell me he loved me and beg me to come back. Then I would deliberate and take my time and keep him in agony. But even during these bad times I realised that I was happy more of the time than not. It had been the other way around when I was with him.

Being alone gives me plenty of time for thinking and I've realised that in my own way I was quite unfair to Oliver. I used to think that I was being patient and understanding, but I was only making a martyr of myself; I used to be so superior about being tolerant, but then got upset because he didn't give me what I wanted. How could he when I never told him! If I had been really honest with myself and with him from the very beginning probably I would never have gone to live with him.

It's not easy being that honest, but I'm practising and on some days I'm better at it than on others.

I'm lucky to be friendly with Marion; since Kathy got married we've become quite close. She keeps encouraging me. Only the other day I was telling her the latest in the Sister Magdalen saga and she reminded me that being your own woman isn't only about dealing with men, there are lots of oppressive women too. Sister Magdalen is one of them and the more I think about her the more I'm sure that I'm going to have to do something about her soon. I'm not sure yet what that will be, maybe I'll just have to leave St Brigid's, but for the moment I'll just concentrate on being as honest as I can.

'Of course you're the liberated type,' an assistant said to me in a shop the other day. It made me think. Am I? I don't know. A lot of the time it doesn't feel like that. I suppose I'm less tied up in knots than I used to be, but then is anybody ever fully liberated? I don't know.